UPSTAIRS, DOWNSTAIRS

"What a foolish, dear lass you are."

"Foolish am I?" she asked. She chose to ignore his use of the word "dear," and the feelings it aroused. He could get the sack for such familiarity, and she suddenly realized she didn't want him dismissed after all.

"Foolish only in the sweetest sense. Your sister is fortunate. Never have I seen such devotion and tender care for another. And from a beautiful young lady who could be the toast of London, but who . . . sacrifices herself . . . gladly. . . ."

He paused. Her eyes drew him like twin vortexes. If he did not move, he would drown in them. But he could not move.

She was without thought. The rhythm of his words, the tender light in his eyes, the beauty of his face . . . these called to her in ancient tongues both unknown and familiar.

Gently, almost unwillingly, he pressed his lips to hers.

Her eyes were full of wonder as she pulled back from the kiss. But as she looked at him shyly, her gaze settled upon his powdered wig, and rational thinking was restored with the force of a thorough dousing of cold water.

"How—how dare you!" she declared. "You have kissed me, Duncan!"

"That's as may be, Lady Druscilla, but you kissed me as well!"

"I most certainly did not! I would *never* kiss a footman!"

"Well, begging your pardon, Miss High-and-Mighty, but you have kissed a footman *now!*"

* * *

"[A] shining talent!"

—*Romantic Times*

My Lord Footman

Marcy Stewart

ZEBRA BOOKS
KENSINGTON PUBLISHING CORP.

For the friends of a lifetime:
Donna Helen Schopke McMillin, Marilyn Anderson,
Libby McCready, and Lynne Peterson

ZEBRA BOOKS are published by

Kensington Publishing Corp.
850 Third Avenue
New York, NY 10022

First Printing: March, 1995

Printed in the United States of America

1

Lady Druscilla Selby was angry.

Seeing her approach, servants dashed into rooms and disappeared.

"Papa!" she called, her voice echoing in the cavernous rooms of Brownworth-Selby Hall. "Papa!"

On the day of Lady Druscilla's birth, her father, who had been inspecting the year's harvest with his steward, had run the length of three fields of barley to greet her.

Now, nineteen years later, Lord William Selby, Earl of Cathburn, honoured veteran of His Majesty's Royal Navy, recent advisor in the Battle of Waterloo and fearless rider to hounds, crept behind the suit of armour in the hall of his ancestral home. Hearing the sound of approaching footsteps he cringed pitifully, but recognizing his butler, he extended an entreating hand.

"Hayes!" he hissed.

"Papa!" The voice grew nearer. "Papa, where are you?"

"Hayes . . ." the earl repeated urgently.

Understanding dawned on the face of the servant, who immediately began to look about him with the air of a conspirator. Lord Cathburn watched him hopefully.

After a moment which seemed an eternity, the butler murmured, "My lord," and nodded toward a large serv-

ing table in the adjoining salon. The earl raced toward
it, gave the servant a doubtful glance, and climbed beneath. When Hayes swept a Kashmir shawl from the
back of a loveseat and draped it across the table's front,
warmth and gratitude for his faithful retainer flooded
Lord Cathburn's heart.

I must increase his wages, he thought. *He is worth
every shilling.*

There was only time for Hayes to amble haughtily
from the room before the earl's daughter reached his
former position. Peering at her behind his screen of
threads, the earl shuddered. Her eyes were sparking like
green fire. Had he stayed with Sir Knight, he would
have been discovered by now.

Lady Druscilla placed her fists upon her hips in a
most unladylike manner, shook her head of golden
curls, and glared at the butler. "Have you seen my father?" she demanded.

Hayes fixed his gaze at a point just above her head.
"Do you mean this morning, Lady Druscilla?"

She snorted indelicately. "Of *course* I mean this
morning, Hayes. I am aware you saw him last evening;
you saw *all* of us then." She sighed and lowered her
arms. "I suppose it is no use becoming angry with you.
It is only that I must speak with him immediately." Her
gaze became speculative. "He becomes harder to find of
late."

"Yes, my lady."

"Well, then." She walked a few paces, moved her
hands restively and paused. "It seems I must ask you.
Hayes, who visits Clarissa in the library?"

The butler swallowed. "Sir Cedric Bottomsby, my
lady."

You should not have told her that, the earl thought
sadly from beneath the table.

"I knew it!" She clenched and unclenched her fists.

"And the doors are closed. She is alone in there with that—that weak-kneed milksop." Lowering her head, she stared up at him through thick lashes. "My father gave him permission to pay his addresses, didn't he?"

"Lady Druscilla, I—" Seldom at a loss for an appropriate and soothing word, the silver-haired butler thought hard for a moment, then shrugged his shoulders helplessly, a thing he never did.

"Never mind, Hayes." She smiled grimly. "I shall handle matters."

Seeing her determination, the servant shivered.

The earl shivered, too, partly because of the look in his daughter's eyes, and partly because his leg had taken a violent cramp and he was like to cry out in pain. Moreover, the dust beneath this table had been begging for the satisfaction of a sneeze for some moments and only the pinching of his nostrils had saved him from discovery. When this was over—if *ever* it was to be over—he must have Hayes speak with Mrs. Crumb about the parlourmaids.

"What—" Hayes paused to clear his throat and cough delicately, "what do you plan, my lady?"

"I plan to support my sister," she said evenly. She turned and walked a few paces down the hall, stopped, then cast a final glance in the direction of the salon. "And you may tell my father I shall be needing that shawl this evening, if he is done with it."

The butler opened his mouth and closed it. Flushing to the roots of his hair, he turned from her searing gaze toward the table, which now bumped and billowed in reaction.

"All for naught, Hayes," moaned the earl as he grasped his servant's hand and attempted to straighten. "All for naught."

Druscilla clicked her tongue in disgust and continued down the hall. Her slippers beat authoritatively against

the Italian marble floor; her long skirts swished in soft
accompaniment. She walked past the little salon, the
drawing room, the small and large dining rooms, the
music room, and the library which, since a visitor was
within, was flanked by two footmen.

A smile began to play about her lips.

She had nearly entered the morning room when she
paused. A gleam of curiosity appeared in her jade-
coloured eyes, and she retraced her steps a few paces.

The footmen outside the library stood at attention in
all their glory: gold-coloured knee breeches, satin waist-
coats embroidered in matching gold, ruffled shirts and
white silk cravats, white stockings and black-buckled
shoes, powdered wigs; all the finery made fashionable
decades ago, the fashion which her father preferred in
his footmen's livery.

Her eyes passed over Jessup, knowing him as she had
since she was a child, but she stared at the tall man beside him with interest. She glanced at his shoes, which
had flat heels, then at Jessup's, which had very high
heels indeed. Still the man towered over him.

And had he looked at her just now? She glanced at
him sharply, but his eyes were staring straight ahead as
they should be.

"You're new," she decided.

His gaze met hers. "Yes, milady."

"Do not look at me when you speak. Hayes should
have told you that."

He looked away quickly, but not before she spied a
glimmer of annoyance in his brown eyes.

"What is your name?"

"Duncan, milady," he answered, turning his head in
the opposite direction as he did so.

"No, do not look *away* when you answer," she said in
exasperation. "You should fix your gaze—oh, I do not

have time for this now. Tell Hayes you need further training."

"Yes, milady," he said humbly, and stared at the floor.

Druscilla frowned. Was the man deliberately baiting her? If so, he was treading in dangerous waters. But mayhap he was only slow-witted, and she had no desire to overtax him. Shaking her head, she walked on and entered the morning room.

When the door closed behind her, Jessup leaned toward his companion and whispered, "You don't want to be flying in her wind, mate. Take my word for it. Stay outta that one's path."

"Is she always this . . . exacting?" he asked softly.

"Ho! Exacting? 'Tis a good word for it!" Jessup chuckled silently, then sobered. "Well, no. She didn't used to be such a nail-splitter, but she has been this past year or more."

Duncan nodded thoughtfully and returned to attention.

Inside the morning room, Druscilla prepared to put her plan into action. She tiptoed toward the door which connected the room with the library. Gently, slowly, she opened it and peered into the opening as far as she dared.

Good. As she suspected he would be, Cedric Bottomsby was waxing eloquent and did not notice her intrusion.

"But Lady Clarissa," he was saying, and Druscilla winced to hear the whining note in his voice, "you are all that I dream of. I think of you constantly. I have always held you in the greatest esteem, even when you were a little child running about the estate, and I a callow youth watching from afar."

Such stuff, thought Druscilla, and wrinkled her nose.

"You are so beautiful, and are such a dear young lady. So kind, so refined."

That is true enough.

"I would not have you think that—that the—recent events make any difference to me. Do not let that enter your mind, no, not for one moment."

Druscilla stiffened.

Clarissa murmured something too softly to hear. Her tone was placating but insistent. Druscilla knew she would be weary now of his futile entreaties but too polite to hurt him. Yet knowing Sir Cedric, only the must brutal of rejections could penetrate his self-important brain.

When Clarissa had finished speaking, Sir Cedric flung his arms about her and drew her to him. While she struggled to free herself, he said heedlessly, "I wish to *care* for you, Clarissa! Surely you are appreciative of that! My mother says I am mad, but—"

"For once I am in agreement with your mother!" Druscilla snapped as she marched into the room. "And I will thank you to remove your hands from my sister!"

Since her voice was loud enough to be heard in the hall, the library doors were immediately flung wide by the two footmen who took postures of dispassionate aggression in the open doorway.

Sir Cedric's arms fell to his sides as he turned his shocked eyes from Druscilla to the footmen. When his gaze registered the size of the new man, his shock turned to alarm, and he sprang to his feet.

"I—I—" He looked back at Druscilla. Seeing her sardonic expression, his embarrassment turned into anger. "Why were you spying upon us? I received your father's permission to be here, I would have you know."

"My father does not know you as well as I do, Cedric Bottomsby. And I was spying, as you call it, for just the reason you have experienced—to protect Clarissa from your pleading and mauling."

He opened his mouth to protest, but she did not give

him the opportunity. "Now do you go, Cedric, I grow tired of you."

"Well!" he sputtered. "I never have—this is quite—" He shook his long, lanky hair. His weak, heavily lidded eyes darted from the sisters to the footmen and back again. When the large footman made a slight move in his direction, he jumped. Taking a deep breath, he gathered the vestiges of his dignity and said, "Good day to you then, Lady Clarissa."

"Good day, Cedric," she answered quietly, and almost managed to disguise the amusement in her voice.

Cedric looked as if he wished to say more, but the looming presence of the footman robbed him of all thought. Pausing only to give Druscilla a look of naked venom, he left.

With a triumphant expression she looked at the footmen and nodded toward the doors. As they moved to close them, she watched the new servant with some appreciation. His protective gestures—not that they had been needed, not with Cedric, she could handle him—had not gone unnoticed.

And then, just as he bowed himself out, the footman glanced upward and met her gaze. She was startled to see the look of humorous complicity in his eyes and the twitching of his lips as he struggled to contain a smile.

For a moment she almost yielded to this sharing of victory, but she resisted and lowered her brows in disapproval. After all, she had *told* him not to look at her directly. It would not do for servants to get ideas above their station. And he had looked at her *deliberately,* she realized, for there was no mistaking the intelligence in his eyes, just as there was no mistaking the look of disappointment in them now as he turned away.

She stared at the door. Why should he be disappointed? Did he expect to be treated as a social equal?

She hoped he would not prove to be a willful servant, for he could be valuable to them.

Now her routing of Cedric felt flat. It was this Duncan fellow's fault, of course, for her sense of disquietude. She must speak to her father about his impertinence.

But Clarissa was speaking, and Druscilla had no idea what had been said. She sat beside her sister and murmured, "I beg your pardon, dear."

Clarissa leaned her head back and laughed, a lazy, throaty sound full of delight. "I *said,* what a heroine you are, Dru! But I should have been quit of him eventually, no doubt."

"Of course you would have been!" Dru said hurriedly. "I merely hastened matters a trifle."

"Poor Cedric," Clarissa chuckled. "Poor, poor man."

Dru looked at her in growing alarm. "You did not—you could not have considered accepting his offer, could you, Rissa?"

Rissa's face immediately became thoughtful. "Well, there *is* his fortune, you know . . ."

"But it is not nearly as much as ours. In fact, I suspect—" Dru broke off and bit her lip.

Lifting her eyebrows, Rissa said, "You suspect he was after my portion, do you? My charms alone are not sufficient, is that what you mean?"

"You have beauty enough for ten ladies," Dru said fervently. "I have never seen anyone as lovely."

Indeed, Clarissa was extraordinarily beautiful, having been blessed with delicate features upon skin so fair and smooth it seemed poreless. Her eyes were a translucent blue, her lips gently curved and rosy and prone to frequent smiles. With thick hair the colour and texture of moonlight, with her regal slimness and feminine manner, she became the focus of any room.

All of which Dru had once resented, for who could hope for attention with such an older sister? She felt dowdy in comparison. Whereas Rissa was tall, she was only of average stature; Rissa's hair was the colour their mother's had been, but Dru's had darkened to burnished gold; Rissa was slim, but her own body was too rounded to be fashionable and would probably run to fat someday were she not careful; Rissa had the complexion of a fairy princess, while her own skin was disgustingly healthy-looking with rosy cheeks and a tendency to turn brown did she not constantly use her parasol.

Of course she had resented her sister, but that was before she discovered Rissa was as beautiful inside as she was out.

"You are wool-gathering again," Rissa chided. "Now, there is the matter of his lands adjoining ours . . ."

"But there is no profit in that since Father does not have a male heir and the estate is entailed, and Cousin Alistair shall inherit the whole," she protested. "You *cannot* have entertained such a notion, Rissa! Cedric is a—a pompous worm! Not only does he bear a strong resemblance to a crow, but even worse, his mouth gathers spittle in the corners when he speaks!"

Rissa laughed unrestrainedly. "What excellent reasons to avoid marriage. Thank you for your wise counsel, my sister!"

The crease which had been growing between Dru's brows faded in relief, and she burst into laughter. "Oh, you have been funning me! Are you not ashamed?"

"Not in the least," Rissa gasped, wiping tears from her eyes with a lace-edged handkerchief.

At that moment the door slowly opened. Lord Cathburn entered, darted a timid glance at his younger daughter, and smiled hopefully. "I heard laughter," he said. "May I share in your merriment?"

Actually, he wished to be in his study pretending to read Herodotus, but he must make amends sometime, and from the sounds emanating from the library, the time seemed fortuitous.

"Do come in, Papa," Rissa beamed.

Dru eyed him with less pleasure. "Please close the doors," she said.

It was an ominous beginning, and Lord Cathburn's heart gave a great thump, but he nodded for the footmen to do her bidding. Thinking he might as well get the worst over with first, he said heartily, "I hear Sir Bottomsby just had his heart broke."

"Well—" began Rissa.

"I don't understand why he had the opportunity," Dru challenged.

"You don't know how the fellow has plagued me this month or more, Druscilla." The earl began to pace. He shook his head of sparse white hair in consternation and linked his hands behind his back. "Couldn't get rid of him, d'you understand? Made no difference to him when I told him Rissa would have no part of him. He wanted to find out for himself. So . . ."

"So you subjected your daughter to his overly familiar advances just so you would be spared the conflict," she sneered.

"Dru," admonished her sister, "you are speaking to Papa."

The earl ignored her. "What do you mean, 'overly familiar advances'?"

"When I entered the room, his arms surrounded her like an octopus. Rissa was fighting him off."

"What! Is this true, Clarissa?"

She shifted uncomfortably. "She exaggerates a little, Papa. Do not become alarmed."

"But he did embrace you against your will?"

"He did," Dru asserted.

Lord Cathburn stopped pacing and drew himself up

to his full height. His face lost its vague look and filled with an angry purpose.

Dru watched the transformation with interest, for she had judged her father a weak man because of his gentleness toward her and her sister. She had not enough experience to know that such gentleness is often a sign of great strength.

Now, for the first time, she was able to believe he *had* been a naval hero in the American Rebellion, no matter that the outcome had been so dismal. Previously she had thought the tales exaggerated, if not entirely fabricated. But *this* was a father she could respect.

"The popinjay deserves a sound thrashing," he said forcefully. "And I'm the man to do it."

"No, Papa!" Rissa pled. "You could be hurt!"

"Let him go," said Dru, eyes shining.

The earl nodded decisively and turned toward the door.

"Oh, Papa," Dru added, "I wish to speak with you about the new footman before you leave."

Groaning inwardly, he stopped.

"I fear he has been impertinent," she said.

"Oh?" He looked surprised. "Impertinent in what way?"

She rose from her seat, walked to the window and pulled back the draperies. Staring nonchalantly into the rose garden she said at last, "He looks at me."

"He . . . *looks* at you?"

"Yes." She glanced at her father and saw he was staring at her as though she had lost her senses. "You take my meaning, don't you? Instead of properly gazing into the distance, he . . ."

"Looks at you?" the earl repeated helpfully.

"Yes, he does! And I have asked him not to."

Lord Cathburn chuckled. "Well, you're a fine-looking

young gel, my dear. Can't blame the fellow." Seeing her face he added hurriedly, "But I will speak to him."

He moved hopefully toward the door.

"And . . . don't you think he is too . . . large, Papa?"

The earl gnashed his teeth, then tried to turn the gesture into a smile. "Too large, Druscilla?"

"Yes. He does not match Jessup at all."

"Oh, that! It cannot matter."

"But I thought you always tried to match the footmen! You have been so concerned with their livery and such."

"Yes, that is true, but . . . I have been thinking of hiring larger footmen. They can carry more packages, walk longer distances . . ."

She blinked rapidly and frowned.

Outside, just beyond the doors which were not as stout as they should be, Jessup eyed his companion apprehensively. Bigger footmen, was it now? And what was to become of proper-sized men such as himself? No doubt it would be fare-thee-well for him, and after years of service, too.

He gave the new man a bitter look. He had thought to like him at first despite his high-toned air, but now . . .

Duncan intercepted that look with a wink. "He is only fobbing her off," he whispered.

"Oh, aye," Jessup breathed in relief.

They straightened quickly as the door opened.

"All will be well," the earl was saying. "And now I shall pay a visit to young Bottomsby." He bustled from the room, hurrying in order to avoid further demands. As he passed the footmen he turned his head toward Duncan and without stopping whispered, "Stop looking at her, for pity's sake."

The young ladies followed more slowly in his wake, Dru with her arm about her sister as though to comfort her still. Deliberately turning her back toward Duncan she said, "Jessup, please inform Hayes we will require the chaise after luncheon to go into town. And do remind him of our engagement at the Winters' this evening."

"Yes, milady," Jessup said to the painting of a stern-faced, bewigged matron hanging across the hall.

The two servants remained immobile until the sisters had ascended the stairs and were out of sight. When he was certain they were gone, Jessup turned to Duncan and rolled his eyes.

"Ladies," he said, and shrugged his shoulders expressively.

"Indeed," Duncan responded with a grin.

That afternoon, Dru and Rissa were driven to town in the four-wheeled chaise the earl had given them in honour of their joint debuts in London. The chaise was white with gold-leaf trim and sported the family's crest—a sailing vessel and a sword, for the Cathburn men had ever turned to the sea in times of their country's need. Dru often suspected this hereditary obsession hearkened back to pre-noble forebears who earned their bread as fishermen and sailors, but even she had never suggested such a thing to her father.

The chaise was pulled by a pair of black mares, lively but not mean-spirited. They pranced along proudly and seemed to enjoy the outing as much as she did.

The day was fine and the young ladies had the top down. Both were fond of the sun's warmth and the whisper of sea breezes against their faces; accordingly, their parasols, virtuously unfurled at the beginning of the journey, now rested against the blue velvet upholstery of the conveyance.

Their destination was Cathburn-at-Sea, a tiny fishing village which was virtually all that remained of the earl's shire, crowded as it was between the borders of

Devon and Dorset. Though the village was small, it contained Daley's Emporium, a shop which had often come to their rescue between their infrequent visits to London.

"I hope you've not pinned your hopes on Daley's overmuch, Dru," Rissa was saying. "There are so many shades of pink."

"Yes, but he's bound to have something that will blend, at least. 'Twill be a shame do you not have ribbons to match your new gown." Dru paused to study several newly shorn sheep grazing in the chalk downs. "I should have had the dressmaker supply them."

"It's hard to remember everything," Rissa said leisurely. With a little sound of pleasure she leaned her head backward and closed her eyes.

She is like a cat, Dru thought and smiled. *So beautiful and graceful, and capable of enjoying the comforts of the moment with total abandon.*

"I trust I will remember Papa's new cane," Dru said. "It should have arrived by now."

A frown appeared on Rissa's brow. "I do hope he is all right. It worries me that he didn't come home before we left."

Warrior lights gleamed in Dru's eyes. "He is doubtless teaching silly Cedric a lesson he will never forget."

The footman's shoulder shook suddenly and drew her attention back to the driver's seat, an area she had tried to ignore during their journey. Earlier, when she had descended the front stairs of the Hall, she'd felt dismay realizing the new footman waited to attend them.

"Why do you accompany us instead of Jessup or one of the others?" she had questioned.

Averting his eyes, he replied the earl had so ordered him.

"But you have not the experience."

"No, Lady Druscilla," he had agreed. "I believe experience is what he wishes me to gain."

Narrowing her eyes, she had looked for signs of insolence in his face, but his expression remained blandly innocent. And then he had made himself ridiculous by trying to place himself at the back of the chaise like a tiger.

"Do go sit beside the driver, Duncan!" she had demanded. "The top is down and I will not have you looming over us in this fashion!"

He had obeyed her with alacrity, and at least had the grace to keep his eyes turned toward the ground. Now, apparently, he had been listening to their conversation and found it amusing. Unless he had a twitch, of course, and she would not be surprised if he did.

She was wondering if it was not her duty to admonish him for this latest infraction when they entered the village. But seeing the cluster of little buildings, many of them formed of white freestone from the Isle of Portland, hearing the cry of seagulls and the voices of fishermen calling to one another in the harbour, and smelling the many flavours of the sea—not all of them pleasant, but sharp and beguiling for all that—she dismissed him from her mind.

"The sea is uncommon peaceful today; the waves hardly disturb the surface," Dru said. "Oh, and there are the Winston-Smythes."

"Truly? Where?"

"Just emerging from Daley's."

As Crickley halted the horses, the young ladies exchanged waves and greetings with these older friends of their father.

Duncan jumped from his perch beside the driver, lowered the stairs, and held out his hand to assist Dru. She placed her hand in his with some reluctance.

For a moment she wondered at herself, that she

should feel this reluctance. Of course, thĕ man *had* tried her patience all day, but she often had problems with the servants when they did not fulfill their duties properly. Yet she did not feel this reluctance with *them*.

At least his grip was strong and sure, and she felt no danger of tumbling on her head. But she could not like the feeling of weakness his strength made her feel. Why, her hand almost trembled in his.

She watched him assist Rissa with a solicitousness that was gratifying to see. And then, noting the difference in their heights, she felt relief. She had felt strange because of his size, that was all. It was natural that such a tall man could make her feel peculiar. She simply was not used to such an experience.

Thus restored, she rushed to link arms with Rissa, and the two walked inside Daley's.

"Wait outside, Duncan," Dru ordered when he attempted to follow. "The shop is no bigger than a dressing room and you will crowd us."

Feeling more satisfied than she had in the last several moments, Dru prepared to shop. A half-hour later, they had selected pink and green ribbons as well as several lengths of cloth for servant's livery. The earl's new cane of carved mahogany had arrived, and Rissa begged to carry it.

"It is wonderful to touch, Dru," she explained. "Do you not like the feel of the carvings?"

Dru agreed and called for Duncan to carry their packages. As she suspected, when he entered the shop he seemed to dwarf it. Mr. Daley happily piled the parcels into his arms, and the footman struggled to balance them as he opened the door.

Rissa exited first with Dru following closely behind. In her delight with the new cane, Rissa thoughtlessly extended it before her onto the sidewalk. Unfortunately, a man was passing by at just that moment, and he tripped and sprawled painfully at their feet. The momentum of his fall jerked the cane from Rissa's hands, and had not Dru been nearby to steady her, she, too, would have fallen.

"Are you all right?" Dru chattered, cradling her sister's face in her hands. "Are you hurt, my dear? I am so sorry, I should have gone first."

The distress on Rissa's face began to ease, though she still shook in reaction. Now she began to soothe her sister. "I'm not hurt, it's all right, Dru."

From the sidewalk the fallen man looked at them in disbelief and began to scramble to his feet. He brushed dust and sand from his rough clothing and tried to restore the previous contours of his hat. When the footman dropped his parcels to comfort the young lady, his indignation could be contained no longer. So this was how the Quality treated strangers in their puny village!

He stamped over and stood in front of his assailant. All right, she might be as pretty as a dream, but pretty would only go so far. Here he stood, and still she ignored him! He was almost speechless with rage.

"Wot are you, blind?" he sputtered at last.

The other one, the little one, turned on him in fury. He had time only to register a pair of dangerous green eyes before she answered him with all the anger of a hissing cat.

"Yes, she is, you terrible man! Now begone!"

His eyes widened in remorse and he began to stammer apologies. There seemed no way to make amends, however, and aside from an understanding look from the footman, he received no absolution, and he slunk off muttering, "Well, 'tweren't my fault."

Before returning for the fallen packages, Duncan assisted the young ladies to the chaise. Rissa had recovered her composure very well, but the eyes Dru turned upon him were glassy with unshed tears.

When his gaze met hers in sympathy, she made no objection.

2

Within her darkened bedroom an hour or so later, Dru removed the damp cloth from her face and stared into her hand-mirror. Excellent. The red puffiness about her eyes had almost disappeared. A few moments more should be all that was required. Rissa mustn't know she had wept. Naturally, she couldn't see the condition of her face, but she would detect the tears in her voice did Dru not recover herself.

Allowing the mirror to slip from her fingers and onto the bed, she plunged the cloth into the basin, wrung out the excess water, placed it over her eyes, and leaned back.

And stared into darkness.

This was Rissa's world now. Complete and utter darkness. There was no respite for her, not ever. Never a holiday from the dark. *Rissa* could not lift off a comforting cloth and have the visual world restored to her.

No, no. She must not dwell upon it. The old sorrow would overwhelm her again. It was much better to feel anger. Anger could be controlled, whereas grief could not. Anger could be directed, but sorrow shook her as a lion did its prey, leaving her weak, spent, helpless.

No, anger was more satisfying. Anger at the rude ruffian this afternoon, who had so crassly reminded them of Rissa's condition (as though Dru ever ceased thinking of it); anger at the unknown beast who had caused her blindness; anger at God, or fate, for allowing the tragedy to happen; and anger at herself, for it was her fault.

Her fault. If she hadn't dawdled at the mirror that day a year ago, Rissa would not have been alone on the London footpath. She would not have been kidnapped, and the accident to her head would not have occurred. Dru knew no one blamed her. Papa and Rissa would doubtless be shocked to know she blamed herself. But she was accountable.

It happened during their third week in London. The Season had begun in earnest, and their long-awaited debut was a success. Days and evenings were a dizzying round of teas, dinners, opera, plays, soirees, routs, and balls.

Rissa, no more eager than was her sister to be married, had delayed her debut a year so that they could "come out" together. It was not a hardship for her to do so, since they had been uncommon close since infancy. Even their court gowns were identical, save that Dru's white satin was embroidered in gold thread at the hem, while Rissa's was edged in silver.

The *beau monde* had fallen at their feet, or at least at Rissa's feet. Dru attributed her own lesser popularity to the overflow of her sister's admirers. Gentlemen were drawn to Rissa's beauty and charm. Before the first week had passed, she had rejected two suitors, one of them a marquis.

And it hurt her to do so, Dru remembered. Rissa had wept after denying each offer. But she longed to marry for love, as did they both, their thoughts on the matter having been formed by many hours of novel-reading.

Of course it went without saying that their future husbands, the two gentlemen fortunate enough to win their love, would be handsome, wealthy, titled, and possessing the disposition of a rake—reformable rakes swept into virtue by the innocence and beauty of their wives.

However, the reality was quite different. The wealthy gentlemen were often old, many of them widowers. Rissa's marquis had been older than their father. The handsome ones seemed more concerned with their own reflections than the ladies they escorted, and the rakes were disgustingly depraved and showed no desire to change. Complicating matters were the fortune-seekers, many of whom were dangerously charming when confronted with a wealthy earl's daughters.

After three weeks Dru was still hopeful, but discouragement grew. She had had her fill of seeing the same faces, hearing the same tiresome gossip (only the names changed), having her thinly slippered feet trod upon by the same overperfumed and underwashed dandies.

It did not help to note that Rissa's admirers seemed a cut above her own.

Every evening began the same way. They would enter the room together—whether it be a ball, musical evening, whatever—with Papa trailing behind; he would rush off to the card room, and gentlemen would begin to gather about them. Civilities would be exchanged in lightly flirtatious tones, someone would make a witty remark, and then Rissa would laugh, or flash her eyes at some fortunate admirer—how devastatingly she could look at one!—and the ranks of gentlemen would swell, and their eyes would look to her, their comments would be directed in her direction, hoping for that laugh, that look, that touch of her personality which drew one so. Dru understood their attraction; there was something magnetic about her sister, and she felt it, too, though heretofore she thought it only the love which anyone felt for a sister. But it was more, it was a power Rissa had, and not one deliberately used; she was genuine, she was sincere, and the more powerful for that.

And as the gathering of gentlemen grew, somehow Dru would become separated from Rissa. It was not a purposeful pushing aside, she knew; the gentlemen weren't unkind, only unthinking. Before long she would find herself on the periphery of the crowd, and if she was fortunate, one of the admirers too far from Rissa would take pity on her or himself and engage her in conversation, or ask for a dance. But many times she would be alone and free to wander about the room sipping ratafia or watching angry mamas whispering to their daughters behind their fans, their eyes piercing Rissa and her court from across the room.

Eventually Rissa would note her absence and look about the room for her. Catching her eye, she'd wave for Dru to join her, but more often than not Dru would shake her head stubbornly and flash a false smile, as though the opportunity to stand alone was the reason she had attended in the first place.

Out of such evenings an ugly thing began to be born in Dru's heart, a thing she had never before felt.

Envy.

Her heart was becoming as green as her eyes.

She fought it, tried to ignore it, determined to overcome it. If she tried harder, she reasoned, the gentlemen would notice her, too. But trying harder only made the rejections more painful. Yet still she tried, for nothing could be worse than the green wall that threatened to separate her heart from her sister's.

She was still trying on the afternoon of the kidnapping. It was the reason she was late.

Rissa, no doubt sensing the growing estrangement, had asked Dru to accompany her on a walk. The earl's town house on Clarges Street was surrounded by the residences of well-known personages, and the sisters often enjoyed strolling along the the footpaths while speculating about the lives of those who lived within.

One such favourite was No. 11, where Lady Hamilton had once lived. Rissa had suggested it as their destination, and Dru agreed.

It was a rare afternoon which held no engagements, and both were conscious of the need to hurry before unexpected callers prevented their escape. But Dru had been dissatisfied with her appearance.

"Are you almost ready?" Rissa had asked from the doorway of Dru's bedroom.

With her eyes on the mirror and her abigail, Dru said, "Pizzy is almost finished with me. I shall be down in a moment."

"I'll await you outside then," Rissa replied. "The day is too fair to waste."

As Rissa turned to leave, Dru glanced at her sister's reflection in the mirror. She wore a white sprigged muslin dress with tiny flowers, flowers of the same luminescent blue as her eyes.

Dru returned her eyes to her own reflection. Her ivory dress looked insipid by comparison. Though the material was finely embroidered with blue and grey ferns at sleeves, hem, and bodice, it did nothing to enhance her eyes and colouring. But within her wardrobe rested a new daydress bordered with emerald ribbons . . .

Dru envisioned the two of them walking together in the sunshine: Rissa in blue, herself in green. A phaeton would pass by with a handsome lord and his equally handsome friend. They would spy the two of them, beseech to make their acquaintance—which they would be too ladylike to allow—and follow them home. After introducing themselves to the earl, they would be allowed to properly pursue their acquaintance, and True Love would be born.

"It was your green eyes," her husband, the duke,

would say on their wedding day. "Your sister is lovely, but when I saw you in that green dress, your eyes fairly leapt at me. Such beauty cannot be resisted, and I have loved you since."

So there was nothing for it but to change her clothing. Naturally, her hair was mussed in the process and had to be repaired. It was a full half-hour later before she hurried down the stairs and out the door.

Rissa was not there.

Dru had looked down the street and around the corner, then returned inside. Hayes was as bewildered as she, for Rissa had not re-entered the house.

Thus had the nightmare begun. An ongoing nightmare of wildly searching servants, magistrates, and Bow Street. Then, the ransom note. The delivery of fifty thousand pounds. And the discovery of Rissa—wan, bruised, mute with terror.

And blind.

In many ways, the nightmare continued still.

Dru removed the cloth from her eyes and sat up. If she thought about it more, she would weep again, and she must be strong. It was the least she could do. Rissa in her sweetness had adjusted as well as anyone could, but even she could not tolerate sympathy or pity. Or guilt.

Walking cautiously in the darkened room, she opened the draperies and rang for Pizzy. It was too early to begin changing for dinner at the Winters's, but her stint on the bed had disturbed her hair and wrinkled her dress.

The maid arrived quickly. Seeing her mistress's condition, she shook her head and clucked her tongue. "Now, you've been at it again, haven't you, dearie?" She guided Dru to the dressing table and began rearranging her hair with plump fingers. Dru submitted quietly to her ministrations. The abigail was of a motherly disposition despite her youth—she was no more than two years her elder—and Dru took an odd comfort in her fussing.

Pizzy sighed heavily. "Oh, it's dark days in this house. Dark days indeed." Dru winced as the maid pressed a hairpin into her scalp. "Oh, sorry, dear. Now, we're going to need the rice powder tonight. You've gone and let little blotches come on your cheeks. I've told you not to go on so. You know Lady Rissa 'twasn't hurt. But then, you've a gentle heart, I keep telling them below, they just don't know you."

Seeing Dru's ironic eyes in the mirror, she clamped her mouth shut.

After a moment, Dru asked, "Has my father returned?"

The maid nodded solemnly. "He has indeed. As I said, dark days, dark days."

"What do you mean?" Dru asked in alarm. "Is he injured?"

"Now, don't lose your feathers. He's all right, but his eye is black as cook's pot."

"What!" The young lady jumped from her chair, almost overturning it. "Where is he?"

Pizzy, hairpins falling from her fingers, took a step back. "Lord Cathburn is in the library, but your dress—"

"A pox on my dress! I must go." She walked rapidly to the door, then turned angrily. "You should have told me, Pizzy."

The maid, crestfallen, stared at her shoes. Dru felt a moment's regret, but her anger and apprehension were stronger, and saying nothing more, she rushed from the room.

She fairly flew down the stairs and into the library, noting even in her rush that Jessup and Duncan had been replaced by Alfred and Jacobs. These footmen might have been twins. There was not a hair's difference in *their* heights.

When she entered, Lord Cathburn laid aside his copy of the *Quarterly Review* and stood. "What think you, Druscilla?" he asked proudly. "Am I not beautiful?"

"Papa!" she cried, dismayed. She embraced him briefly, stretched her fingers toward his injured eye, then, fearing she might hurt him, dropped her hand. The bruise was blue rather than the black Pizzy had painted, and it extended downward to his cheek.

"Cedric Bottomsby deserves to be shot," she said. "I should like to shoot him myself."

"Druscilla! Don't talk so." He walked back to his leather wing chair and sat, motioning to the nearby loveseat. When she seated herself, he said, "You've not the idea that *Bottomsby* gave me this beauty, have you?"

"You mean he didn't?" she asked, bewildered. "How, then?"

He grinned sheepishly. "I did go to his house with my horsewhip on the ready, but when I got there, I couldn't get past his mother. You know what she is, Dru."

An unwelcome vision of a complaining, overbearing, vulturelike woman dressed perennially in black entered her mind, and she nodded.

"So, in my disappointment, I er—" he coughed pathetically and darted looks at his daughter, whose brows were beginning to lower suspiciously, "I decided to visit Mrs. Tweetle," he finished rapidly.

"Mrs. Tweetle," she repeated with scorn.

He rose carefully from his chair, walked to the window, and folded his arms across his chest. "Mrs. Tweetle is a highly respected widow, child. Can't think why you seem to take her in dislike."

She thought of Mrs. Tweetle, whose name suggested a plump, kindly, matronly lady who perhaps wore spectacles, baked pies, and took jars of jam to the sick. Instead, she was fashionable, attractive in a sort of blowsy, overblown way, and possessed sleepy-looking eyes which seemed to fascinate her father. She was also a good fifteen years younger than he.

Thinking of her and her drawling voice, her manner so sweetly acquiescent, Dru said, lips curling, "I? I seem to take her in dislike?"

"Appears that way. Anyhow, I, er—I was just leaving her first-floor parlour when I slipped—must have been a bald patch in the carpet—and, er, fell against the newel post." He looked at her hopefully. He dared not add all the truth, that in his attempt to give Dorothy a farewell kiss, he had stepped too far backward and sprawled down the stairs like the most awkward of schoolboys. "Stupid accident, what?"

She stared at him, narrowed her eyes, but decided not to pursue it. "I'm only glad you weren't hurt seriously."

"I'm a bit sore, so can't go to the dinner tonight. Might spoil their appetites to see me, anyhow."

"I'm sorry. The Winters are gracious hosts. Does Rissa know about your accident?"

"Yes, her door was open when I came in, so I visited her. And of course, I told her."

A year ago they had promised Rissa they would never hide anything from her of a visual nature, and though the temptation was strong to protect her, they had agreed.

"How is she? Has she recovered?"

He looked solemn. "Afraid she has one of her head-aches, Dru. Looks as though you'll be going alone to-night."

"Oh, Papa," she said in distress. "I must go see her. And I shan't go to the Winters's either, not without her." She stood and walked toward the door.

The earl limped after her as fast as he could. "Druscilla," he said, and his voice was so serious she stopped in surprise. "Wait. Come back and sit down a bit."

She returned reluctantly to the loveseat. While the earl seated himself beside her, she watched him with an impatient curiosity. He seemed to have trouble beginning, for his eyes grew large and looked in every direction but her own. Finally he said, "I think you should go."

"No," she said firmly, shaking her head. "No, I couldn't, not with Rissa ill."

"But there's not a thing you can do for her, Druscilla," he persuaded. "You know the physician has said the headaches are not serious, not related to her—" He swallowed hard. "Her disability. 'Tis merely a—a reaction to such events as this afternoon, the kind of thing many ladies experience. She'll be given her medicine and will sleep; in the morning she'll be right as rain."

"You know how I feel about Dr. Aaron's diagnosis," she snapped. "He calls her headaches a nervous complaint. Rissa is *not* nervous."

"Naturally she is not!" He enfolded her hands within his own. "Listen to me, Druscilla. You must—you must stop mothering your sister. 'Tis not good for you nor her."

She pulled her hands away and said angrily, "I do *not* mother her. But she needs protection, you know that!"

"Not as much as you're giving her!" He pushed trembling fingers through his sparse grey hair. "You are suffocating her, Druscilla!" Seeing her face, his eyes mirrored the pain he saw in hers. "Forgive me, dear, but you must be told. Take this morning for an example—"

"Yes, do! Had I not been there, what would Bottomsby have done, I wonder?"

"There were two footmen outside the door. She had only to call out."

Dru rose and glared downward at her father. She took a deep breath, started to speak, seemed unable to find words. Finally, hurt replaced anger and she said, "Has she said anything to you?"

"No, dear," he said, and stood up to pat her shoulder gingerly. "But I'm not wrong. And I know she wants you to go this evening; she said as much to me earlier."

She lifted her chin. "I shall see for myself." Mustering her dignity, she passed from the room while her father watched her, sadly shaking his head.

Dru trembled and fought tears as she walked to her sister's room. "Suffocating her," indeed. Her father was capable of the most silly nonsense.

But Rissa was sleeping peacefully when she looked in. Martha Freecastle, her abigail, sat beside her knitting with the energy of a demon. When she looked up to nod at Dru, the needles did not pause.

Dru returned to her room thoughtfully. She had no desire to attend the function now, but perhaps she should go, if only to prove to her father that she did not *suffocate* her sister with unwanted hovering.

Sighing deeply, she rang for Pizzy.

Lord Cathburn's eyes were admiring when Dru descended the stairs that evening. She wore a peach satin gown with a high, stand-up collar trimmed in ivory lace; the same lace edged the front of the gown from collar to hem and decorated the puffed sleeves. A matching ribbon was interlaced among her short curls, and around her shoulders she wore the Kashmir shawl that had offered such poor protection for her father that morning.

He kissed her hand. "You're a sight to make a father proud," he said. "Though you'll be well protected, I'm sorry I cannot escort you."

He took her arm and walked with her to the carriage.

When she saw the footman waiting by the carriage door, however, she stopped suddenly, causing the earl to stumble in an effort to avoid trodding on her feet.

"Papa!" she whispered. "Why is he here? I've no need for a footman; the groom is sufficient."

"Duncan's a good man; he will escort you to their door since I cannot," he said firmly.

With a sinking heart, Dru recognized that rare tone of voice which mean her father's mind would not be changed. She accepted his assistance into the carriage with bad grace, looking sideways at the tall footman as she did so. He wore a pleasantly bored look as though he'd heard none of their conversation.

At least he is learning fast, she thought.

It was fortunate the journey to the Winters's was short, since the presence of the footman outside annoyed her mightily.

Harry and Lady Cynthia Winters lived in a manor house just past the border of Dorset. When the earl's conveyance pulled to a stop in their circular drive, the windows of the rambling old Tudor were cheerfully lit, and carriages lined the drive.

When Duncan opened the door, Dru took a deep breath and placed her hand in his. The walk to the house had never seemed longer. She held her head high and pretended to stare straight ahead, but in truth she darted frequent glances in his direction. Her eyes seemed to have a mind of their own. It was most irritating.

Duncan was all that was proper. He matched his pace to hers and kept her hand securely on his arm. He did not look at her once.

For some reason, that too, was annoying. She was relieved to enter the house.

The Winters met her at the door with warm greetings and expressions of disappointment that Rissa and the earl were ailing. The couple had not been married long.

Though Dru's acquaintance with Harry was lifelong, she had quickly grown fond of his quiet wife, who was also an earl's daughter, and whose shy beauty was not diminished by the spectacles she wore.

Cynthia took her hand and led her into the drawing room. All of the expected guests had arrived. Dru recognized everyone: Thomas Rodgers, a taciturn country squire and his wife, Judith; Emily Lumquist, an aging spinster and acknowledged eccentric; James Burke, their occasional neighbor in Cathburn; and the vicar and his wife, Paul and Lynnette Petersham, and their two marriageable-aged daughters, Claudia and Ceile.

Dru had just finished her greetings when there came a noise from the hall stairs, and a gentleman entered.

"So sorry to be late; I should have left London a day earlier," he said. "I thank you all for allowing me time to change."

Dru looked at him and was lost.

She had thought the footman tall, but the stranger was at least his height. He was extremely handsome with blue eyes, a straight nose, and generous mouth. A blue superfine jacket molded to his strong body, and tan pantaloons fit like a second skin over legs scandalously well-shaped. His cravat was faultlessly folded into a white linen shirt, and his hair gleamed golden in the candlelight.

Her heart raced painfully. For the first time since Rissa's accident she acknowledged herself to be attracted to a gentleman. But this would never do. Something would be wrong with him; he'd be a fortune-seeker, or a gambler, or something worse.

Harry said, "I'd like to introduce my friend, the Viscount Sebastian Montgomery. We've known one another since Eton days."

Greetings were exchanged all around. Dru noted that Ceile's face was the same red as her hair, and Claudia frantically batted her eyelashes at him from behind her fan.

Conversation was general until dinner was announced. The viscount's gaze had caught hers more than once, and she hoped he might take her in to dinner, but it was James Burke who claimed her arm.

"How are you and your lovely sister?" he asked.

Struggling to maintain civility, Dru answered that they were fine.

"Such a sad thing which happened to her," he said softly, turning his large, hazel eyes upon her. "I've been in America this year, as you probably know, and have only recently heard."

Dru recalled that he had once made an offer for Rissa, and fighting down the irritation she normally felt at being reminded of her sister's condition, she murmured noncommitally.

"I trust she has adjusted? That she still finds pleasure in life?"

She looked at him sharply as he held her chair. She found his questions intrusive, but suspecting his concern was genuine, she swallowed as irritable retort and said, "Clarissa is an extraordinary person. She is as she always was. What would have driven another person mad has only enhanced the beauty of her character."

He smiled slowly, his gentle, handsome face taking on a kind of radiance. "Well said, Lady Druscilla. I would have expected as much from her. But how fortunate she is to have such a loyal sister."

She smiled briefly and sat down. The other guests were also taking their seats, and she was disappointed to see the viscount sat beyond conversational reach, having been claimed by his hosts.

Soon they were partaking of the first remove, a clear soup garnished with bits of clam and vegetables.

"I saw Napoleon Bonaparte t' other day," Emily Lumquist announced baldly.

Ceile dropped her spoon into her soup, spraying her bodice and her sister's with broth.

"You—you *ninny!*" Claudia protested, and dabbed frantically at her dress. A footman moved toward her with a fresh napkin to assist, but realizing the location of the stains, he hurriedly withdrew.

"Never mind," Mrs. Petersham said cheerfully. " 'Tis a clear soup, and will come out in the wash."

Claudia scowled down at the blotches on her tucker, glanced in the viscount's direction, saw he was not looking, and made a sideways movement under the tablecloth.

"Ow!" Ceile screeched.

"Saw him plain as day," the elderly lady continued.

Dru watched the viscount's eyes open wide in curious amusement as he looked from Miss Lumquist to the Petersham girls. His gaze caught hers, and she smiled in response.

"What was he doing?" Harry asked solicitously.

"Escaping. Just as he did at Elba, he was escaping from St. Helena's." She nodded her head wisely. " 'Twill happen. My visions always come true."

"You are a visionary, Miss Lumquist?" asked the viscount. His voice was as golden as his hair, Dru noted with pleasure.

"She is indeed," Lady Cynthia said as the spinster stared modestly at her soup. "She dreamt Harry would find a fair-haired wife in London, and . . ."

"And he did," Lord Sebastian smiled. "He is a fortunate man." While Cynthia blushed, he added, "How remarkable of you, Miss Lumquist."

"Perhaps Miss Lumquist is influenced by her memories of last summer," added the vicar, who had no patience with visions, which he regarded as springing from the devil. "Who can forget the *Bellerophon* and Plymouth?"

There were several nods at this stirring of memories. During the previous July, an imprisoned Napoleon and his entourage of forty persons had anchored for days at Plymouth while officials argued his fate. As he waited, over a thousand boats of the curious surrounded the *Bellerophon*, hoping for a glance at the impious Corsican.

"In my vision he wore a green uniform with red facings," Miss Lumquist intoned, trancelike. "Two plain gold epaulettes uponst his shoulders, a white waistcoat and breeches, military boots, the Grand Cross of the Legion of Honour over his heart."

" 'Twas exactly how he was dressed on the ship," the vicar said dryly. "She saw him, as most of us did."

"She's right, though," Thomas Rodgers said unexpectedly. "He will escape." Having gathered everyone's attention, he added, "We all do, in the end."

The table fell silent in glum contemplation of the truth of this remark. Fortunately, the arrival of marinaded pork, roast turkey, and pigeon pies restored everyone to more cheerful thoughts.

After dinner, Dru was pleased to note the gentlemen did not dawdle long over cigars and port before rejoining the ladies in the drawing room. The Winters had several card tables set up for those so inclined, and the doors to the garden were open.

Having no desire for cards, Dru urged James, who seemed to feel she was his responsibility, to play his rubber of whist, and she wandered toward the garden. Lanterns had been lit and hung upon poles. Square beds of red and white roses formed a checkerboard pattern within the paved walkway.

She was just wondering if she might make an early evening of it when Cynthia joined her. "I hope you are enjoying yourself?" she asked.

Dru looked toward the garden, which stretched the entire length of the house. "Yes. Your garden is lovely."

"Not as lovely as the ladies within it," a golden voice said gallantly.

Dru turned gladly toward the voice. She'd not dared to hope he might join her here.

"It would be my pleasure to escort you ladies about the garden, if you wish," the viscount added.

Cynthia looked at him fondly, then glanced at Dru. "I must be about my hostessing duties, but perhaps Druscilla . . . ?"

Hoping she would not appear overly eager, Dru murmured, "I should like that."

As Cynthia returned to the house, the viscount offered his arm and they began to walk. He smelled faintly of cigar and soap and projected a great strength.

They exchanged glances and smiled. He did not seem inclined to talk. Dru listened to the sound of his boots meeting the walk in sturdy crunches. As the silence lengthened, she cast about her mind for something amusing to say, but only the most boring thoughts surfaced. He was sure to think her a great lump did she not speak soon.

When she spoke at last, he spoke at the same time, and they both laughed. The viscount urged her to go first and she said, "I only asked if you had taken part in the war."

"Yes, I was in the Hussars." Upon further urging he admitted that he'd been a major before selling out, then added sadly, "Many of my men were lost at Waterloo, some of them great friends of mine. It's tiresome to speak of it a year later, I know, but nothing is ever the same after such a tragedy. Yet one goes on."

She thought of Rissa and agreed sadly.

They had reached the end of the garden. Steps led downward to the lawn, which was more dimly lighted.

Iron benches circled the occasional oak and ash tree, and islands of bluebells, primrose, sweet pea, and amaranth scented the night air.

Thinking she really shouldn't, she nodded when he suggested they continue their walk.

"The war can be impersonal," he continued. "A soldier takes his orders and goes about his daily life never seeing the generals or officials who may order him to his death. It's easy to lose sight of what one is fighting for. Though I did once see Napoleon." He looked at her and gave a small laugh. "Why I'm going on about this, I've no idea, except that you're such a gracious listener."

After a brief pause he added, "Did you see Napoleon? When he was anchored in Plymouth last summer?"

"No," she said quietly. "My sister was ill."

He was silent a moment, then said, "I'm sorry. It has only just come to me. Your sister is Clarissa, is she not?"

"You know her?"

"I believe I once saw her at Almack's. A beautiful young woman. Everyone wanted an introduction. But I was paying court to another lady at the time, so . . ."

Dru felt an immediate flare of jealousy, then chided herself. Of course he would have many lady friends. After all, he was masculine perfection.

"I'm so sorry about what happened to her," he added. "It must be hard for you, too."

"For all of us." As she contemplated her slippers, he took her hand and moved closer.

"You're a very caring and beautiful young lady," he said.

Dru's heart beat faster. She looked up to find his eyes watching her with a soft expression. Her thoughts flew into confusion and she looked away. Her gaze roamed from the house to the garden, to the shrubbery, to the footman hiding within the shrubbery, to the—

Eyes wide with disbelief, she looked at the shrubbery again. Yes, it was! It was most definitely Duncan watching her and the viscount!

With a look of surprise, the footman immediately crouched down.

Lord Sebastian looked over his shoulder. "Is something the matter?" he asked, and turned back to her.

"What? Er—no," she answered, not sure why she was unwilling to divulge her servant's embarrassing behaviour. "I—I—"

Her eyes grew larger as she saw Duncan's face cautiously rising again from the holly. When he flashed a large grin, she choked until the viscount was moved to pat her back helpfully.

"I—I'm sorry," she gasped. "I must go. My father will be expecting me."

"I hope I haven't offended you," he said in concerned tones.

"Oh no, of course not!" She grabbed his arm and began to walk rapidly toward the house, dragging him as far from the footman as possible. Lord Sebastian allowed himself to be led, though he looked at her in bewilderment.

Just before entering the house, she managed to drop behind him a pace and spied the footman running desperately toward the front. A grim smile appeared on her lips.

Seeing it, Lord Sebastian felt chilled. What had happened to the sweet and understanding young lady of a moment ago? Well, perhaps her father was overly protective, and she was undone at the thought of worrying him.

He placed his hand over hers. "May I call upon you, Lady Druscilla?" he asked.

"Pardon? Oh yes, of course," she said distractedly.

In the ensuing rush to gather her reticule and shawl, she hardly noticed the looks of pure hatred on the faces of Claudia and Ceile as they watched her with the viscount.

She said her goodbyes as quickly as possible. When the butler opened the door, she saw that Duncan awaited her. Since the Winters and Lord Sebastian stood watching, she took the footman's arm as though nothing were amiss. When she reached the carriage, she turned and waved cheerfully. They returned her wave, and after a long moment of continued waving, finally closed the door.

She stared at the footman, fuming. His wig was askew and showed glimpses of thick auburn hair beneath. His cravat was soiled, and there were grass stains on his knee breeches. His cheeks were flushed and his breathing was only now becoming steady—all the running, of course.

While she studied him, he kept his eyes to the ground, but she noted a muscle moving rapidly in his cheek.

The driver and groom looked down curiously from their perch. She narrowed her eyes at them and they looked quickly away.

"Well," she said evenly. "Open the door, Duncan."

He did so speedily, his relief obvious at being let off so easily. She accepted his assistance into the carriage and settled her skirts. Just as he was about to close the door, she held out a restraining hand.

"Now do you come inside, Duncan," she said. "You have some explanations to make."

His shocked eyes met hers, then looked upward to the driver and groom who looked just as shocked, but very interested.

"Milady," he said, a pleading note in his voice.

"In here," she said firmly.

With a final glance of desperation at the driver's seat, he entered the carriage.

3

The carriage jerked into motion. Duncan shifted uncomfortably and ran a finger along his neckcloth. In the pale light of the moon, Dru's eyes pierced him like jade daggers.

"I am waiting, Duncan," she said calmly.

"Milady?"

"Do not try my patience," she snapped. "Why were you watching me?"

"Watching you?" Daringly he met her eyes. "Is that what you thought, Lady Druscilla?"

"I suppose you have another explanation for your presence in the holly bushes."

"Yes, I do." He looked at his hands. "But I'm afraid you will laugh."

Her lips tightened into a thin line. "Do not let that concern you."

"All right, then," he said, and shrugged as if to say it was none of his affair. "I was chasing a rabbit."

"A rabbit," she breathed. In the dim light, he saw her eyebrows lower dangerously.

"Yes, milady. A . . . baby rabbit. For Jessup's daughter Hildy. I saw it bound past the carriage. One of the dogs was chasing it. Hildy's a bonnie wee lass and loves animals, so I thought of her."

"You were rescuing a bunny." She stiffened, and every line of her body shouted disbelief. "I suppose if I asked Crickley and Harris, they would support this . . . story?"

He looked at his feet. "Well . . . the truth is—"

"Yes, the truth, please," she said between clenched teeth.

"The truth is, they were away from the carriage at the time."

"I see," she said, lifting her chin. "How very . . . convenient."

"No, milady, it's not so uncommon. Several of the drivers and grooms were tossing dice while they waited. It tends to get dreary, waiting."

"I daresay. And of course, the . . . bunny . . . unfortunately escaped your rescue attempt."

He smiled at her, his even, white teeth gleaming in the moonlight. "Why no, milady," he said. "He did not."

And so saying, he pulled a tiny, trembling, brown-speckled rabbit from his pocket and offered it to her.

She drew in her breath sharply. Of a sudden, all her anger melted away. No more immune than was the average female to animal adorability, she held out her hands and took the bunny to her lap. Without removing her gaze from the rabbit she said, "I'm afraid I owe you an apology, Duncan."

"That's all right, Lady Druscilla." He crossed his arms and leaned back comfortably. Looking up, she surprised an expression of amused satisfaction on his face, an expression he quickly masked.

Suspicion darted across her mind, but she dismissed it. How could he have conjured a rabbit were he not telling the truth? Still, his posture was hardly servile, and she frowned.

"You are a Scotsman, Duncan?"

He paused. "Half Scots and half English, milady."

"I hear it only slightly in your speech."

"I was educated in England."

"Oh? How fortunate for you to have had some schooling. Although I've heard it said otherwise, I feel it's advantageous for servants to be able to read and write. You attended one of the many charity schools, I imagine. Was it in London?"

The footman uncrossed his arms, and she became conscious of a terrible quiet. "Actually," he said at last, "I attended Harrow, and later, Cambridge."

She burst into laughter. "How amusing you are!"

The bunny quivered and looked about wildly.

Duncan remained a solid and grim presence as she laughed. Recovering sufficiently to notice, she said, "Surely you don't expect me to believe such a tale!"

After a long pause, he said, "No, milady."

She was conscious of an uncomfortable feeling, a feeling like shame. But how irritating for a servant to make her feel so!

Heatedly she said, "If you had the funds for such an education, why would you be in service as a footman?"

"Is there something wrong with being a footman?"

"No, there is nothing wrong with being a footman, and your tone is insolent. I merely wonder why you would not use your education—if indeed you have such an illustrious one as you claim—to become a clerk, or a solicitor or something with a little more ..."

His lips curled. "Societal standing? Prestige?"

"Well, yes."

"Enlightened people are becoming less concerned with social ranking, have you noticed?"

"No, I have not, unless you refer to the scandalous riots which are springing up around the country. I do not consider that enlightened behaviour. Not when the rabble breaks the windows and furniture of decent citizens and frightens old ladies living alone!"

"But if the rabble, as you call them, are starving because of low wages and unfair tax laws, do you find it hard to blame them?"

While they glared at one another, the coach drew to a stop. Dru was surprised to see they had arrived home.

Before he could move to open the door, she said angrily, "I will forgive your presumption this evening, because I suppose it is my fault for taking you into the carriage. Such a thing will never happen again, I assure you."

He opened the door, jumped out and lowered the steps. Waves of anger pulsated from him. When she accepted his assistance—a thing she could not refuse in her long skirts, not unless she wanted to end this evening by rolling head-first from the carriage—her gloved fingers burned as though touching live coals.

She stared upward into his angry, disappointed eyes. *Why is he disappointed?* she wondered, for the second time that day. Was it because she was not "enlightened" in her views? Well, she thought no differently than any other noble English lady on that subject.

It didn't bother her if he was disappointed. His opinion was beneath notice. He was, after all, only a footman.

When he offered his arm to escort her into the house, she stepped aside. "Here," she said, and handed him the furry, squirming bundle. "Here is your bunny." And raising her chin, she marched toward the house alone.

Dru did not sleep as well as she'd intended after her triumph at the Winters's, for triumph was what it had been. Not only had James Burke shown his growing interest by giving her soulful and lingering looks, but the handsome viscount had asked if he could call.

She should have spent the night dreaming of gallant suitors, but instead had been haunted by memories of gently burred speech and angry brown eyes. She was shocked at herself for allowing him to disturb her so, and had scolded herself the whole restless night through.

After breakfast, the sisters went for their morning walk. Rissa had recovered from her headache and questioned Dru in flattering detail about her evening.

"Lord Sebastian sounds a paragon," Rissa smiled. "But he would have to be, if he is to be worthy of you."

"Nonsense," Dru replied, and looked about her happily. "The baby sparrows are stirring from their nest, Rissa, and the leaves of the giant oak look dry. There are unfortunate few clouds, so the prospects of rain are not promising."

They continued in the same vein for awhile, Dru acting as Rissa's eyes, Rissa turning her head in the indicated directions and smiling at the sensations of sun, warmth, and wind upon her face. Sounds accompanied their walk: labourers calling to one another from nearby fields, birds and insects twittering and tweeping, the crushed gravel beneath their feet thudding softly at every step.

As she often did, Dru tried to imagine a world without vision. Rissa had told her the loss of sight had enhanced her other senses, that she was able to hear sounds and savour tastes more keenly than before.

Dru hoped it was enough.

They stopped at a bench and rested for awhile. Dru sat at a vantage point which allowed her to see the Hall in its entirety. Built in the middle of the last century and designed by Inigo Jones, it exhibited the influence of the Italian Renaissance style. Clean, horizontal lines were broken by long, multi-paned windows set in parallel rows; great square towers balanced the west and east ends of the house. It was an impressive edifice, yet it was ridiculously large and required the labours of many servants.

But she did not want to think about servants.

After several moments of silence, Rissa asked, "Did Papa mention to you that he visited Mrs. Tweetle yesterday?"

"He did."

Rissa laughed. "You're not overfond of her, are you, Dru?"

"To be blunt, no. Are you?"

Rissa cocked her head thoughtfully. "She seems a nice lady, and very fond of Papa."

"Fond of his title and riches, you mean."

"Oh, how you go on. It's just possible, you know, that someone could love him for himself."

"I don't deny that. But Mrs. Tweetle . . ."

"Do you never think, Dru, how it must be for him, not having a son? To think that prim cousin Alistair shall inherit the house and lands?"

"I know. It's galling to contemplate."

"But Papa is young enough to have more children, if he were to wed someone as youthful as Mrs. Tweetle. Maybe he would have a son."

"Heavens!" Dru exclaimed, scandalized. "What an idea!"

Rissa turned toward her and reached for her hands. Dru immediately clasped her fingers and watched her sister struggle for words, her brow wrinkling in concentration.

What I would give to have her eyes meet mine once more, Dru thought. *She could speak volumes in a mere glance.*

"I belive that Papa *would* marry again if he had not

the care of us," Rissa said. "I think he hesitates for fear that we would be unable to bear a stepmother."

Dru withdrew her hands slowly and stood. "Surely not. You are mistaken, Rissa."

"No one could ever replace Mother in our hearts, and he knows that. But she has been gone for four years now, and I know he is lonely. I think he hopes we will wed so that he may proceed with his life."

"No, that cannot be. He loves us!"

"Naturally that is so. But witness his allowing Cedric's proposal to me. And recall the lawyers who have appeared of late, and his futile attempts to break the entailment. I fear, Dru, that we stand in his way to happiness."

Dru stared at the Hall, her thoughts churning. She could not deny her sister's logic, but the prospects were hurtful to contemplate. She had always assumed she had the security of her home for as long as she needed it. And of course she still had; but if Rissa were correct, it was at the cost of her father's dreams.

With some bitterness she reflected that twice in the past twenty-four hours she had been informed that her presence was unneeded. First, her father accused her of suffocating her sister; now her sister asserted they prevented their father from the joys of marital bliss.

"Perhaps we should ask him if marriage is what he truly desires," Dru said. "And if so, we could—" she swallowed carefully, "we could tell him he has our blessing."

Rissa laughed softly. "Do you hear yourself? You can scarce say the words, dearest. Do you truthfully think you could live in the same household as Mrs. Tweetle?"

Dru closed her eyes. "Yes, I—well, that is . . . What is the alternative?"

Rissa leaned forward and smiled. "Something very dreadful. One of us should wed, dear sister, and provide a home for the other. And since I must be judged a liability, my hopes are on you."

"No one could ever judge you a liability!" Dru protested. "But I take your meaning."

Suddenly she thought of the tall, imposing presence of Sebastian Montgomery.

"You are smiling, Dru," Rissa grinned. "I can feel it."

"I'm only thinking that perhaps I should increase my efforts in a certain quarter."

"The viscount?" Rissa asked hopefully.

"Oh, yes," Dru agreed, a gleam in her eye. "The viscount."

They passed by the stables on the walk home, for Rissa wished to visit her horse, Satin. Since the accident, she had only ridden a few times, but never Satin. The spirited black was not judged safe enough to be walked on a leading rope.

Crickley was forking fresh hay into the stalls when they entered, and he nodded to them. "Satin's been lookin' for ye, Lady Clarissa," he called jovially. "Wants his apple, he does."

"It's a good thing I happen to have one in my pocket then," Rissa rejoined.

Dru led her to Satin's stall and watched as the black accepted her sister's gift. He seemed to enjoy the accompanying pats and soft words as much as the apple, for he nodded his head and snorted as though to say, *Yes, I must indeed be the finest horse that ever lived, for who am I to disagree with an earl's daughter?*

Noting two unfamiliar grooms brushing the earl's bay, Dru reflected that her father was hiring new servants at a whirligig's pace. And then another man entered at the far end, a tall man with chestnut-coloured hair. Even without the wig and the livery, even in the plain dark trousers and open-collared shirt of a labourer, he was easily recognizable.

Dru watched him approach the two grooms and speak to them quietly. They nodded, spoke some more, nodded again. There was no doubting the submissiveness of their postures. It was as though he were their master.

But that was foolishness.

Still, she watched them with a troubled fascination.

As though feeling her gaze, he turned. Patting the horse's flank, he took on the appearance of a casual visitor to the stables, an off-duty footman looking for something to do. He laughed (falsely, she thought), said a few parting words (the two men answered with uproarious laughter; could anyone be that amusing?) and ambled in their direction.

"What is wrong?" Rissa asked, sensing the growing disquiet in her sister.

"The new footman approaches," Dru said under her breath.

Rissa's face lightened. "Is it Duncan, then?"

"Yes, Lady Clarissa," he said, smiling. He turned his gaze to Dru, and though the smile slipped somewhat, he said, "Lady Druscilla."

"Good day, Duncan," she said frostily. "I perceive you have no duties in the house today."

"It's my half-day, milady."

Hoping to dispel the puzzling tension in the air, Rissa said, "How do you like my horse, Duncan?"

"A fine animal, milady. He has some life to him, that's for certain. A real beauty."

"Yes," she said softly. "How I miss riding him."

"You've not ridden him, then . . . in awhile?"

While Dru glared at him, Rissa said, "Not since my accident, no. It's one of the hardest adjustments I've had to make. We were such partners, Satin and I. Riding him was like riding the wind."

"And you don't ride now at all?"

"Upon occasion a groom will lead me on one of the calmer horses, and we walk about. But not so often anymore."

"And you, Lady Druscilla?" he asked, his golden eyes ignoring the anger in hers. "Do you like to ride?"

"There is not the time to do much riding," Dru said crossly.

"Druscilla won't ride because I cannot." As Dru opened her mouth to protest, Rissa continued, "She'll deny it, but it's true. No effort on my part has ever changed her mind. She sacrifices her own pleasure for me."

If it had not been for me, Dru thought, her eyes beginning to fill, *neither of us would have had to sacrifice anything.*

Duncan looked thoughtful. "Have you never ridden double, Lady Clarissa?"

"Such a thing is too dangerous," Dru snapped.

"Not if she rides astride." He turned toward Rissa. "You could ride the wind again, milady. I myself would be happy—"

Dru said wrathfully, "You forget yourself, Duncan!"

Rissa extended her hand appealingly. "No, it sounds wonderful!"

At that moment Jacobs, looking harried and spent, rushed into the stable and informed Dru that a Viscount Sebastian Montgomery was in the library, and was she receiving visitors?

Dru felt an immediate lifting of spirits, and Rissa urged her to hurry and freshen up, stating Duncan would escort her to the house. Too excited to argue, Dru rushed away.

She slipped in by way of the servants' entrance and used the back stairs to her room. Pizzy was frantically summoned, and within minutes, adjudging herself presentable enough, Dru ran down the stairs, slowed her steps, and entered the library with admirable decorum.

Dru was pleased to find her father and the viscount talking as though old friends. As she curtseyed, they both rose and bowed with gentlemanly deference.

Lord Sebastian was striking in a bottle-green waist-coat, green- and red-striped vest, white breeches, and black boots. Dru thought he looked extraordinarily handsome.

"I've really come upon a double mission," the viscount said, directing his comments to the earl. "First, the Winters have asked me to extend an invitation to your family to attend a musical evening Thursday next. Secondly, I would like to invite lady Druscilla to go for a ride in my phaeton this morning before the day becomes too hot, if she cares to join me and you permit."

Dru cast a look of appeal in her father's direction, and he gave his permission with unflattering rapidity. As to the musical evening, he was sure they would be delighted to attend.

A few moments later, Lord Sebastian helped Dru climb aboard the phaeton. It was not easily done, the phaeton being one of the sportier models which elevated the driver's bench far above the ground. When the viscount snapped his horses into motion, the sight of the earth speeding by so far below made her dizzy.

"Did you bring your phaeton all the way from London?" she asked when her stomach had settled.

"My man did. Harry wanted me here for his dinner, and I knew I must ride fast. But Jack wasn't far behind, since he was aware I might require the phaeton. He's a good man, Jack, and willing to drive through the night."

"He drove night and day? Without stopping?"

"I don't often require it of him. But he was able to complete the journey in twenty-four hours."

"Twenty-four hours!" London was over a hundred miles away, and the distance took them several days.

He looked at her and smiled. "He doesn't mind, Lady Druscilla. It's what he's paid for."

Perhaps Jack fears he will lose his position if he doesn't do as he's told, she thought. And then wondered why she suddenly considered a servant's feelings.

Blinking away an image of brown eyes, she reminded herself to be charming, and suggested a scenic road that paralleled the Channel. "Rissa and I used to ride along it, and there are smooth sections where we raced our horses through the waves," she said.

The viscount was willing, and after turning in the indicated direction, he glanced over his shoulder and said, "Is your father very protective, Lady Druscilla?"

"No more than most, I suppose," she said, puzzled. "Why do you ask?"

"I ask because it appears we are being trailed, and I thought the man might be one of his grooms sent to chaperone us."

It had better not be Duncan, she thought in a sudden fury, and turned to look behind them. But it was not. Though the man was far away, she recognized him as one of the new grooms. When she returned home, Papa had some explaining to do. The viscount might regard such vigilance insulting.

Sensing her mood he said, "It's understandable. I am a stranger, after all."

"And a good friend of Harry's, whom we've known since Adam."

He gave her an amused look and changed the subject. "Do you enjoy music, Lady Druscilla?"

"I like listening. But Rissa is the musician of the family. She plays the pianoforte beautifully."

"She will enjoy the visitors at the musical evening, then. The performers are mutual friends of the Winters and mine, Lord Mason Trentley, Cynthia's stepbrother, and his wife, Charity, who is accounted a fine harpsichordist."

She sensed a withdrawal and looked at him curiously.

After a moment he stared down into her questioning eyes and thought how beautiful she was. Her eyes reminded him of the sea. Her golden curls, ruffled by the wind, tumbled about her face in charming disarray. *Could she be the one?* he wondered. *Will Druscilla be the one to heal my heart?*

But Dru's eyes had grown round with shock. Suddenly becoming aware of the sounds of pounding hoofbeats, he followed the direction of her gaze and pulled to a stop. Along the surf, a man and woman rode astride a magnificent horse. Clumps of sand flew beneath the great beast's strides; splashes of water sprinkled upward to dot the clothing of the riders, and they laughed, uncaring. The man was tall and strong and had his arms firmly about the woman. She rode crouched forward, her fingers entwined in the horse's mane, her riding dress billowing outward to expose a shameful glimpse of ankle and calf, but she was unheeding; her hair streamed behind her in silvery currents, her faultless features were upturned in a beatific expression of joy.

She was a vision. Lord Sebastian's heart began to race. He envied the man sitting behind her.

Dru felt a stabbing pain in her heart. How closely Duncan held her! But that was so she wouldn't fall, of course. What cared she how closely he held her? The important thing was Rissa.

"Rissa!" she screamed.

So this is Clarissa? thought Lord Sebastian, spirits suddenly falling. *But she is blind.*

Duncan saw them and began to pull on the reins, to Rissa's obvious disappointment.

"Rissa, pray come into the carriage this instant!" Dru

demanded when they had reached the phaeton. "You could have been killed, as Duncan should know!"

Rissa's eyes turned in her direction. Her face still wore a kind of rapture. "I have ridden Satin again, Dru," she said happily. "How wonderful it is."

"I know, but it is too risky. How dare you, Duncan! I vow you shall be sent packing for this piece of work today!"

Rissa's expression became stubborn. "That he shall not. I ordered him to take me."

"I find that hard to believe, since I stood by you when he suggested such a ride."

Duncan said, "She is safe with me, milady. There is no danger."

"How can you say such a thing! There is every danger!"

Lord Sebastian said mildly, "It appears she is unharmed, Lady Druscilla. Perhaps, since she enjoys it so much . . . ?"

Dru felt the threat of angry tears prickling behind her eyes. The injustice of it! Everyone stood against her, even the viscount, who looked at her cautiously as one might view a madwoman. And all she wanted was to assure the safety of her sister.

Of a sudden she recalled her father's words. Was this what he meant when he accused her of overprotecting Rissa? She had no desire to *suffocate* her with unwanted caution.

Though her heart trembled with imagined outcomes, Dru forced her lips into a smile and said, "I must admit the sight of you on Satin is one I've sorely missed. You looked beautiful riding him." Which was true enough, though with her hair falling wildly about her shoulders, she looked a hoyden; whatever would the viscount think?

She is like a goddess arising from the sea, Lord

Sebastian was thinking. *Her eyes, though sightless, appear to be without depth. One could become lost in the reflecting emotions of her eyes.*

With dawning hope Rissa said, "You don't mind, then? I may continue to ride?"

For a moment Dru could not speak. Her heart was pierced by the submissiveness of her sister's questions. How could she now deny the truth of her father's statements? She *had* been ruling Rissa's life, so much so that Rissa had waited until Dru was out of the house to ride covertly; now she begged permission to continue, as though Dru were her mother. And this from a sister who once had all London at her feet.

Wiping at her eyes, Dru said, "If that is what you wish. After all," she added, forcing a laugh, "you are the elder and don't require *my* permission."

Rissa's face was transfixed with joy. "Then let us ride on, Duncan!"

"Wait!" Lord Sebastian shouted, half-rising from his seat. Then, realizing the extremity of his reaction, he grinned sheepishly and said, "I believe we haven't met."

Dru apologized and made introductions. After a few moments of pleasantries, Rissa's impatience became painfully obvious, and Duncan reined the horse away.

"Do you be careful, Duncan!" Dru called after them, not entirely able to relinquish a year's watchcare all in a moment.

They watched until the riders were tiny dots on the horizon. Then the viscount turned the phaeton about, and they began the journey home

Neither spoke much. Lord Sebastian was preoccupied with thoughts of Neptune's daughter, and Druscilla kept recalling the look Duncan had given her before riding away.

His strange, golden eyes had been soft with approval. She didn't really care how he'd looked at her; it was just refreshing to see something other than disappointment on his face, that was all. It was the novelty.

In fact, the novelty was so interesting that, when the groomsman pulled from beneath the tree to follow them home, she scarcely remembered to be annoyed.

4

"Hop-hop, little Thilver," sang four-year-old Hildy Jessup. "Go hop-hop pleath." She placed a chubby hand beneath her rabbit's rump, but the animal, being disinclined to move from his warm bed of hay, only gave her a stubborn look.

Karl Jessup leaned back from the table to watch his daughter. "She's that fond of her new bunny, ain't she, Meg?" he said.

His wife poured tea into the earthenware mugs she'd been given as a wedding present by the earl and stirred warm milk into one of them. Sighing heavily under the weight of a long-hoped-for second pregnancy, she sat down.

"She is. That were sure a surprise."

Jessup knew she didn't refer to their daughter's enjoyment of the rabbit but to the gift itself. "Oh, I dunno, Meg. He were quite taken with our Hildy." They watched as the rabbit began hopping industriously about the cottage. "There he goes, Hildy!"

"Yeth, I know!" the child giggled, pressing her tongue gleefully into the space left by two missing teeth. She held up a long needle of straw. "He din't like thith!"

"You're raisin' a hellion, Meg Jessup," he said proudly.

"If she keeps gettin' spoiled by the likes o' that Duncan, she truly will be."

"Oh, don't go on so. He's a real brick, he is. Even if he do talk like an upper."

"That's wot I can't understand. Wot's a man like him doin' here? He's too high in the instep, Karl. Somethin' ain't right."

He sipped his tea and set the mug down firmly. "Don't go gettin' nonsense in your head, woman. Mr. Hayes, now, he talks fine; and Jim Jacobs had him four years o' schoolin'."

"Jim Jacobs has sheep's liver for brains," she said scornfully.

He snorted. "Magdalen Spencer Jessup, I'll be taking you over my knee do you not mind your tongue."

Since he was not a violent man, they both laughed at the impossible mental image he'd conjured. "I wisht you would," she panted. "Mayhap you'd bring on this lazy child." She patted her swollen stomach and looked pained.

"He's just takin' his time is all. Ain't no hurry."

"Easy for you to say."

They sat comfortably for a few moments. Hildy, tiring of making her rabbit jump, scooped him from the floor, wrapped him in her doll's blanket, and took him to the rocking chair.

"I still think somethin's up," Meg said. "He just don't fit in. And wot about them other new men? The earl's not had that many groomsmen, stableboys, and gardeners since I knowed him."

Jessup shifted his weight in the wooden chair and pursed his lips. He was remembering a sight which hadn't meant much at the time, but in the light of Meg's suspicions it now seemed sinister. Two days before, the

earl had asked him to carry a scratched and worn footstool to the attics. On his way Jessup had passed Duncan's room in the servant's wing. He'd been surprised to
hear voices within the room, since Duncan should have
been on duty, and he decided to investigate on his return. But when he emerged from the attics, it was to see
several men leaving the room with Duncan trailing behind. They hadn't seen him, and since all went about
their stations, he'd said nothing. But now, upon reflection, it did seem odd that all of Duncan's visitors were
new men.

Meg had been married to Karl for a long time.
"You're thinkin' o' somethin'," said she.

"Naw, Meg," he said gruffly. "Just got to get on duty,
is all." He rose from the table and stretched mightily, a
portrait of unconcern.

Meg looked at him shrewdly and sipped her tea.

Lord Cathburn put his feet upon the ottoman and
sighed contentedly. The chair in which he sat was of no
particular style except comfortable, and its ancient
crewelwork had long ago faded into flattened blotches
of indefinable colours. Mrs. Tweetle had a fire going in
the grate despite the season, and its warmth was welcome, her little house being shaded into winter by a
multitude of chestnut, oak, and eucalyptus trees. Little
pots of flowers scattered scent about the room. The
brass fittings of the fireplace shone like mirrors; reflections of flames danced in the polished mahogany of the
occasional tables. On the round table before the window
was an embroidered cloth spread with the remains of a
satisfying luncheon: thinly sliced chicken and ham
sandwiches with crusts removed, several varieties of
cheeses, petit-fours, sweetmeats, and his favourite, fried
apple tarts.

He had a great love for this expanded cottage, so different in its warmth and homeliness from the vast spaces of the Hall. The earl was a simple man who enjoyed simple pleasures; were it not his duty to rattle about and oversee his ancestral home and occasionally fulfill military and political duties, he would have found the life of a country squire more to his taste.

Inextricably wound into his fondness for domestic coziness was the lady sitting opposite him. The firelight from hearth and candle highlighted her white hair and softened the faint lines beneath her eyes. He thought she looked very distinguished sitting there, studying her book. Distinguished enough to grace an earl's home, without doubt, even if she didn't have a drop of noble blood within her.

Virginia Tweetle felt his glance and looked up from her copy of *The English Garden*. She smiled at him, her brown eyes softening, as she wondered what he was thinking. Hopefully he thought her attractive in her violet dress. She knew the dress's colour contrasted strikingly with the premature white of her hair, her greatest vanity. Made of velvet and trimmed in Irish lace, the dress had a high collar from which the material fell away to reveal an expanse of still-youthful bosom. The dress was of her own design and perhaps more suited to evening wear, but in her experience, gentlemen were less concerned with the appropriateness of a garment than with its enhancement of a lady's better qualities.

She had grown mightily fond of the earl since he had begun visiting her during the past year, though she was unsure if she loved him. In her youth she'd known the kind of love which could toss one from the mountain peaks to the valleys, all in a moment, but that had been her husband, Samuel, who'd been lost at sea. What a fine, strong man he'd been; tall and handsome with a thick head of black hair. Not at all like the dear earl with his thinning, grey-streaked brushwire hair, his portly middle, and, it must be admitted, his small stature which forced her to walk slightly bent at the knees in order to avoid the appearance of towering over him. But with the earl there was a sense of comradeship that she could not remember with Samuel, who was much the my-lord-and-master kind of man.

During her ten years of widowhood there were many gentlemen who'd taken an interest in her, though once they learned she was unwilling to slip beneath the sheets to solace her loneliness, most turned to easier prey. But there had been offers, too. None of them were able to ensnare her heart, for she enjoyed her independence; and having sufficient funds left her by a spinster aunt, she was able to live a comfortable, if not extravagant, lifestyle.

But Lord Cathburn was different. They shared similar interests, and the earl considered her opinions as he would those of an equal. Moreover, as she neared the end of her child-bearing years, she began more and more to feel the lack of children. When the earl spoke of his frustration in not having a son to inherit, she could not help thinking of the possibilities. However, when she recalled the haughty eyes and ways of his younger daughter, the daydream stiffened and crumbled to dust.

"What are you thinking about, Mrs. Tweetle?" asked the earl. Though their companionship had grown as comfortable as tea pouring into a cup, they had never used one another's given names.

"I'm still thinking of forming a Zodiac garden," she said, which was not entirely a lie, since she had been thinking of it before looking up from her book. "With one colour for each of the signs. It would be intriguing to relate colours appropriately, do you not agree?"

"Sounds heathenish to me," he said doubtfully, shaking his head. "You'll have Vicar Petersham around your neck, I warn you."

"But it's merely an excuse to have a circular garden with many colours; 'tis not as if I believe in the Chaldean arts. What think you of white primulas and potentillas for Capricorn?"

"I think you'd do better to call it a clock garden and have a colour for each hour. Save red for four o'clock, for that's tea-time and my favourite hour."

She laughed gently and set the book aside. "You seem uncommon happy today."

"I've had a good week, Mrs. Tweetle. Clarissa hasn't had one of her headaches in days, and dashed if Druscilla isn't acting better towards her. Not so stifling. Even permits her to ride Satin with the footman." Now if she would only stop pestering him about the man, things would be almost perfect. Wanted him to sack Duncan, that was plain, though she hadn't said so in words. Suspicious little baggage, was Druscilla, he thought with some pride. Though he'd never admit it to anyone, his spirited younger daughter had ever been his favourite.

"Clarissa has been riding Satin?" Mrs. Tweetle asked, her heart quivering for the earl's beautiful, flawed daughter.

"Now don't you start, my dear. She's safe as a sighted person with Duncan. Good man, that."

Mrs. Tweetle hoped he was right. She had a great fondness for the child. If only Druscilla would show a measure of warmth toward her as Clarissa did, there might be a future for the earl and herself.

"Is Clarissa riding today?" she asked worriedly.

"No," he said, and rubbed his arm, which was still sore from the tumble down Mrs. Tweetle's stair. "No, today 'tis a picnic with Lord Montgomery and the Winters."

"Lord Montgomery seems a frequent visitor."

The earl scratched his nose proudly. "That he does. Takes quite an interest in our Druscilla. Seems a fine lad. Always includes Rissa on their outings, too, which is wise of him, since there's no quicker way to Dru's heart." He gave her a look of undisguised hope. "Might be hearing wedding bells sometime soon, Mrs. Tweetle. Can't be sure, of course, but things are heading in that direction."

May it be so, she prayed silently, and smiled into his eyes. But she said nothing, because there were things understood between them that could not yet be voiced.

The earl returned her fond look with one of his own, and found to his surprise that the back of his eyes felt scratchy. In order to hide this unmanliness, he said in a gruff voice, "Druscilla better keep on her good behaviour. I won't have her getting into one of her mad tizzies and shying this one away."

Please God, he added reverently. *Don't let anything set her off.*

Dru brushed an ant from her skirts and clenched her teeth. The footman's actions seemed to be bothering no one else, and nothing could be gained by making a scene. Still, she had a few words impart toward him once they were alone. The audacity of him!

The outing had begun nicely enough; the Winters's large carriage had accommodated the five of them comfortably, and even Duncan's presence had not overconcerned her, since he rode with Jessup in a second carriage containing the picnic paraphernalia. They had driven to a sparsely wooded area overlooking the channel only twenty minutes away from Brownworth-Selby Hall. Finding a grassy spot that was suitably flat but still allowing of an admirable view of the water, the gentlefolk had left the picnic preparations for the footmen and wandered down to the sea. There they daringly removed shoes and stockings and waded among the waves.

So much had been pleasant, and Rissa had delighted in the sensations of foam and sand; even the pebbles scarcely bothered her. Lord Sebastian had taken to escorting them both, one lady on each arm, and though Dru was on the landward side and consequently had the driest feet, she could not regret it when exposed to Rissa's constant merriment. How good it was to have the attention of an exemplary beau who was willing to make her sister feel admired and appreciated again. It was only a little step to imagine a lifetime of such comradeship and mutual esteem.

Lord Sebastian would never balk at Rissa's living with them once they were wed, Dru was certain, and surely he would offer for her soon. She could not have overestimated his feelings for her, for whenever he called, a special light appeared in his eyes, and his manner was decidedly courtly. And the frequency of his visits revealed the intensity of his interest; since their first phaeton ride, not a day had passed without a visit from the viscount.

Of her own feelings she gave little thought. Such an admirer was a compliment to her femininity; his presence was comfortable and always pleasant. The three of them found many subjects of mutual interest and humour. If her heart did not race and jump like a frog on a griddle when he was around, well, that proved nothing. She'd been led to believe love would cause such a reaction, but her only sources on the matter had been the writers of romances, and they probably knew no more about the subject than she did.

So the morning had passed enjoyably until it was time for luncheon. They all pulled on stockings and shoes again, as modestly as possible, and Dru was only slightly discomfited by the traces of sand which grated between her toes. But as she approached the picnic site, a heaviness settled upon her. It was the same whenever she saw Duncan. She could not understand it, but it was so.

He'd now taken Rissa for three rides on Satin, and she had to admit that her sister's love of these outings had done wonders for her. Dru accompanied them on their last two rides, and Duncan had been a quiet and subservient presence, only speaking when required. But his answers and comments were undeniably intelligent and smacked of good breeding. Dru was beginning to believe he *had* been educated at Cambridge, and she found that impossible to reconcile with his present position, no matter what his arguments otherwise. There was something *sinister* about a man who would waste himself so. If indeed he was only a footman.

Rissa's experience had forever changed Dru's view of the world. Before the kidnapping, the world had been a safe place: predictable, sane, loving. Now she knew there were other possibilities. It was not difficult to form suspicions when one's security has been shattered. Particularly when the villain's identity had never been discovered.

Though she could not imagine Duncan in the role of a kidnapper, there were other nefarious reasons for an impoverished gentleman to pass himself off as a servant.

It didn't help to see how easily he insinuated himself into the household. He'd certainly won Rissa's loyalty when he re-introduced riding into her life. Even worse was the hold he seemed to have over her father. Whenever she questioned the earl about the new footman's background, or how he came to hire him, he'd brush her off with some light answer that told her nothing. And more than once she'd seen Duncan entering her father's study to converse with him privately. It was all very mysterious and trying, and she could imagine no good coming from any of it.

At least her suspicions, vague as they were, offered an explanation for the anger and discomfort she felt whenever Duncan was near.

She'd tried to dismiss those feelings during their luncheon. Both Duncan and Jessup had served the meal faultlessly. Small folding tables had been arranged to form a buffet table, and the footmen served their plates as directed. After settling themselves on cushions, each guest was served champagne in fluted glasses. It was all very elegant and correct. Until Rissa invited the footmen to sit with them and partake of the meal.

"But why should they not join us?" she'd asked when Dru made an objecting noise. "There really is no reason. Jessup is like one of the family, and Duncan has surely earned such a small reward by his masterful handling of Satin."

Lord Sebastian's back stiffened. Dining with servants was a shocking idea. But suddenly he remembered another lady who had similar egalitarian thoughts; she'd once brought her maid to Vauxhall with them. He'd lost that lady, perhaps in part because of his inflexible standards. Now he said quickly, "Yes, do let them join us. There is plenty for all."

While Harry and Lady Cynthia looked at one another in astonishment at this uncharacteristic behaviour, Dru fumed. It seemed she was destined to be subjected to the footman's presence at every turn.

That Duncan was pleased by the invitation, there could be no doubt. But poor Jessup trembled as he placed a few random items on his plate. He sat on a far corner of the blanket and said not a word. Not so Duncan. He joined into the conversation like a relative.

Which made Dru so angry she could scarcely speak. The presumption of the man!

And now he was speaking of Scotland as though he were one of them. To make matters worse, the others attended him with expressions of rapt interest, even Lord Sebastian. It would be better did they not encourage him.

"The Highlands are known for the roughness of the terrain and climate, but the people are hardy," Duncan was saying. "So many lochs, bays, and firths; mountains savage in their heighth and roughness—how could such a land not breed hardiness into its people?"

"And that is where you were born?" asked Cynthia.

"Yes, milady."

"How do people live in such a harsh land?" Harry wanted to know.

"There is the usual farming, sir, and fishing, both in the North Sea and the firths. The salmon fishing is excellent for sport or livelihood. And of course," he added, his eyes twinkling, "there is whiskey."

The men murmured reverential agreement to this statement, Dru noticed with a jaundiced eye. Even Jessup forgot himself long enough to nod, though his eyes darted about as though following bees.

"Such a land is full of mystery," Duncan continued, his voice lowering for effect, his accent becoming more pronounced. "It is a land of legends, of tales handed down from father to son before the hearth on a winter's evening. Tales of Norsemen, of battles brave and vicious; stories of wraiths and lost souls torn from their lovers."

"Tell us one, Duncan," Rissa breathed.

"I don't know, milady," he said with a reluctance so false that Dru pursed her lips together in disgust. "If there be any faint-hearted ones here . . ."

Everyone, excepting Dru, rapidly denied such a possibility.

Duncan cast her an amused glance and continued. "This tale was reputed to happen at Balconie House in Cromarty in the last century. You must imagine the land in its wild splendour, for this is a place of deep gorges, waterfalls and caverns unexplored, where flows the River Allt Grand in all its terrible might."

He set his plate aside and leaned an elbow on his knee while they watched him, transfixed. Dru noted cynically that he now avoided looking in her direction. "When the Laird of Balconie brought home his bride, she was unaccustomed to the land, but enchanted by it. She became possessed by the call of the gorge, and went to it separately, day by day. On the final evening, her maid accompanied her. Suddenly a spirit, a man in green, appeared. The lady linked her hand in his, walked to the edge of the precipice, and jumped."

"How very sad," Cynthia said. Her eyes were large and dreamy behind her spectacles. "Did her husband ever find her?"

"No, never, milady. But here is where the legend begins. Years later, a fisherman claimed to have discovered her chained within a cavern; a sad, living captive to the evil man in green. When the townspeople searched, she was not to be found."

Despite herself, Dru shivered. When Duncan glanced at her, she recovered sufficiently to give him an annoyed look.

"We have a ghostly tale near here, too," Harry said. "In Lyme Regis. Many years ago, a carriage and horses and all within it simply disappeared. On the highway where it's said to have happened, noises can be heard from time to time. Noises not unlike the sound of horses pulling a carriage."

"In Kent, there is a castle which was once a Roman

fortress," Lord Sebastian said, not to be outdone. "There is a story that a Roman guard fell to his death from one of the towers. Dwellers in the castle often hear footsteps climbing the tower stair, but never descending."

Jessup gave the party a wild look and jumped to his feet. "M-more champagne?" he asked. His nervousness caused them all to laugh, and while he bustled about filling glasses, there was a general relaxing of positions. Dru watched him hesitate when he approached Duncan's glass; Jessup, at least, realized the inappropriateness of the situation if no one else did. But Duncan gave him a friendly wink, and Jessup filled his glass.

The Scotsman had power over everyone, evidently— excepting herself.

Cynthia shivered playfully and said, "I love to hear ghost stories. It's frightening, but in an easy way. It's not as if such things really happen."

"No," Harry agreed, "most often there is a simple explanation for eerie occurrences. The wind rubbing two branches together can sound frightful. The mist might resemble a human body on a moonless night. That sort of thing."

"It is the occurrences of the real world that are most frightening," Rissa said soberly. "Just when things seem most ordinary, when one goes about planning the day's activities, and the next day's, everything might change, all in a moment. And then there is no going back to the way things were before."

Everyone fell silent. Sad looks were sent in her direction. Dru moved her cushion closer to Rissa, took her hand, and pressed it to her cheek.

"You speak of your tragedy," Duncan said gently. "We all of us share in your grief. There is no accounting for the random events which may happen to the most innocent of victims."

Dru gave him a vitriolic look and bristled. Sensing it,

Rissa lifted her free hand, warning her away. "Thank you, Duncan," she said. "One of the hardest things is that no one wishes to speak of it. I've not wanted to myself, until lately. But now . . . it's difficult to explain, but . . . I constantly feel the need to discuss it, to . . . to understand it, if such a thing is possible."

"I didn't know, dearest," Dru said, and lowered Rissa's hand from her cheek to enfold it within her own.

Lord Sebastian's eyes were overbright and fixed intently upon Rissa's face. *How sweetly he cares for her,* Dru thought, looking at him. *It's as though she is his sister already.*

"The strangest thing to me is not the kidnapping," Rissa said, a puzzled look upon her face. "I think I can understand, though never condone, such an act. No doubt the man was penniless and felt he could not earn such a large sum of money, no, never in his life. I cannot know what drove him to such an act of desperation—"

"And cowardice," Dru added succinctly.

"And cowardice," Rissa continued, her lips twitching, "but he had descended to the depths. What I cannot understand is how a *gentleman* could have done such a thing."

"A gentleman!" Dru squeaked. "Whatever can you mean, Rissa?"

"Well, perhaps not a gentleman, but a man who was well-educated. I have been dreaming lately, Dru, dreams that have reminded me of something I'd forgotten." Rissa removed her hand gently from her sister's and pressed her fingers to her temples.

"Is your head hurting you?" Dru asked. "If so, you must not speak about it now."

"No, there is only a little pressure, not like one of the bad headaches, and I do want to continue." She lowered her hands and sighed.

"Your dreams, Lady Rissa . . ." prompted Duncan.

"Yes. But first, in the event anyone here does not know, I should explain that my blindness was an unintentional result of the kidnapping." She took a sip of champagne and winced as though it were medicine. "When the hansom cab pulled up beside me in front of our town house, an elderly voice hailed me and asked for directions to a haberdashery on Bond Street. I thought it strange at the time, for why would the driver not know its location? Still, the voice was querulous and helpless all at once, very pathetic-sounding, so I walked nearer the cab to give what assistance I could. Soon I realized I had been deceived, for a youthful figure, masked, leapt from the carriage, tossed a blanket over my head, and pulled me toward the carriage door."

"Is there anything about him that you remember, Lady Rissa?" Duncan asked. "Anything that might identify him?"

"No, for I struggled greatly, and the next few instants are confused. At some point the blanket fell from my head and I achieved my freedom momentarily, but when he grabbed me once more, the blanket became entangled under my feet and I fell toward the pavement. I believe I hit my head either upon the curb or the cab's wheel, and after that I lost consciousness."

Dru put her head in her hands. She could hardly bear to listen, but if Rissa needed to talk about it, she must. Directly after the tragedy, her sister had told the story over and over to magistrates and Bow Street runners, but she'd not spoken of it since.

"When I awoke, there was darkness all around me." Rissa stopped a moment and lowered her head. When she tilted her head upward again, a glaze of tears covered her eyes, tears which she rapidly blinked away. "I thought I was in a dungeon, but then I noticed little sounds that told me I was not alone. I felt the warmth of a lamp near my head. The person guarding me was moving around, setting out food from the odour of it, and his movements were sure, not those of someone groping about in the dark.

"I realized that I was lying on a bed, unbound, and I sat up and put my hands to my head, intending to remove the blindfold, for surely that was what caused the darkness. But there was no blindfold. When I knew at last that I was ... blind, I ... well, I can't remember a great deal after that."

Cynthia murmured sympathetically while Dru wiped tears from her eyes. She'd foolishly forgotten her handkerchief, and Duncan handed her his own. Dru hesitated only a moment before taking it. Giving him a curt nod in thanks, she glanced up and was surprised to see he watched her with kind eyes.

"It is this part I have dreamt of during the past days," Rissa continued. "This ... confused state of fever, weeping, drifting. Through all of it, I was treated well. That he'd not expected such an event was apparent, and I knew he was sorry. He never ... harmed me in the ways in which a rougher man might have; I was always treated with respect, and even gentleness.

"But he disguised his voice. The entire time, he spoke gruffly, as a ruffian might. All along, all this past year, I've thought he must have been as he sounded. But in my dreams I've heard another voice, and now it has come to me that it is the kidnapper's real voice. Not that I can remember it plainly enough to describe it to you, but there was one time, just when he realized I was blind, that he was shocked into using his true speech. And the cadence of his words was that of an educated man."

"Can you remember what he said?"

"Yes, Duncan, I can now, for I've heard it in my dreams. He said, 'Oh, God, this cannot be true, I am so sorry, Clarissa.' "

"He knew you," Duncan breathed.

"The devil!" Lord Sebastian said angrily. "Death would be too easy for such a villain."

"But," Cynthia said diffidently, "surely he would have discovered Clarissa's given name. Does it necessarily follow that he was personally acquainted with her?"

"It is possible he did not know me," Rissa said slowly. "But I think he did; otherwise, why disguise his voice? Beyond that, there was something ... familiar about him."

Dru stumbled to her feet and fled toward the trees.

"Dru?" Rissa said worriedly. The others watched the retreating figure in concern, and Lord Sebastian was almost to his feet when the Scotsman rose.

"If you will permit me, Lord Montgomery," Duncan said, and hurried after her without waiting for permission.

The viscount shrugged his shoulders and reseated himself beside Rissa. "I'm certain she's all right," he said, and pressed her hand comfortingly. "The footman will bring her back when she's recovered. No doubt she's overset by your story, as I am."

"As we all are," Cynthia said.

Rissa smiled wanly. "She is too gentle-hearted. No one has a more caring sister."

The viscount thought it might be so, but he'd never known anyone to possess greater courage than this young lady sitting beside him, not even on the battlefield. This beautiful, charming lady. It was a joy just to look at her, so much so that he forgot he still held her hand until she gently reclaimed it.

Misinterpreting the strange look on her face, he said, "Don't worry. Duncan will fetch her shortly. He seems a good man." And he could not help adding, "If a trifle forward, considering his position."

The good man was having some difficulty finding Dru. He hesitated to call for her, since the others might fear she was well and truly lost. In the end it was the sound of weeping that drew him; he found her sitting atop a fallen log, her shoulders hunched over and wracked by great heaving sobs.

At the sight of his despondent little adversary, he felt his heart melt. Knowing full well she might snap at him for his insubordinance, he sat beside her on the log and said, "Och now, lass. Dinnae go on. What's done is done, and your sister's a fine, brave lady who still has a full life with much joy ahead, and the love of her good family to comfort her."

Dru turned her tear-soaked face toward him, a face overcome by joy, Duncan noted in shock. "It is not my fault," she chanted. "Rissa's blindness is not my fault!"

"But—of course 'tis not your fault, Lady Druscilla! How ever could it be?"

"She was waiting for me on the footpath, don't you see?" Dru chattered feverishly. "I told her I'd be down directly, but I changed my dress and took ages to meet her. When I finally arrived, she'd been stolen!"

"I still don't understand—"

"You don't? All this time, Duncan, we've thought the kidnapper was a common ruffian, someone of the lower classes."

He paused. "I know you're prejudiced against such folk, but I don't follow your reasoning."

She made a face at his allusion to her class consciousness. "I've always felt that the kidnapping was an impulsive thing; that the criminal was roaming about in the cab looking for an easy way to obtain money. I thought he might have been searching for an empty house to rob when he spied Clarissa standing there. And that if I had been there, he would never have tried to steal two ladies."

She wiped her face with Duncan's handkerchief. "But now, horrible as it sounds, it appears Rissa knew the kidnapper. I can't be happy about that, but it does mean he must have planned the whole thing; if he had not abducted her that day, he would have at another time. So it is not my fault!"

Duncan looked down at her beaming face and felt his chest constrict. "So all this time, you've borne this guilt?" When she nodded, starry-eyed, as though it had been nothing, just a mere trifle to carry the weight of her sister's blindness upon her shoulders, he said, "What a foolish, dear lass you are."

The smile faltered and she raised her chin. "Foolish, am I?" she asked. She chose to ignore his use of the word "dear" and the feelings it aroused. He could get the sack for such familiarity, and she suddenly realized she didn't want him dismissed after all.

"Foolish only in the sweetest sense. The kidnapping couldn't have been your fault even if the situation had gone the way you'd imagined. I tell you, lass, your sister is fortunate. Never have I seen such devotion and tender care for another. And from a beautiful young lady who could be the toast of London, but who . . . sacrifices herself . . . gladly . . ."

He paused. Her eyes were round with fascination; they drew him like twin vortexes. If he did not move from this log, he would drown in them. But he could not move.

She was without thought. The rhythm of his words, the tender light in his eyes, the flushed beauty of his face . . . these called to her in ancient tongues both unknown and familiar.

They leaned toward one another. Duncan gave her a searching look, his eyes serious and expectant. His gaze dropped to her lips. Gently, almost unwillingly, he pressed his lips to hers. It was a tender kiss, a caress soft as rose petals, her very first.

Her eyes were full of wonder when she pulled back from the kiss. Strange sensations were coursing throughout her body; she felt as though a giant had seized and shaken her like a child's rattle. It was not an entirely unpleasant feeling, and one she was willing to experience again; but as she looked at him shyly, her gaze settled upon his powdered wig, and rational thinking was restored with the force of a thorough dousing of cold water.

"How—how dare you!" she declared. "You—you have kissed me, Duncan!"

In the space of a heartbeat the Scotsman's emotions plummeted from the sublime to injured despair. Turn on him like a hellcat, would she? Well, two could play that game.

"That's as may be, Lady Druscilla, but you kissed me as well!"

"I most certainly did not! You are a *footman!*"

"Thank you for reminding me of my chosen occupation, but what that has to do with anything, I wish I knew."

"It has *everything* to do with it, as well you know. I would *never* kiss a footman!"

"Well, begging your pardon, Miss High-and-Mighty, but you have kissed a footman *now!*"

"Oh!" So enraged was she, and so run out of arguments, she did a thing she'd never thought to do. She raised her hand to slap him.

It was not going to be a very hard slap, Dru decided all in an instant. Just enough to teach him his place. But he saw the hand coming and captured it within his own. She struggled to remove it, but he was having none of it; he didn't trust her, that was evident. So she brought her other hand forward in defense, and he caught that

one too, and there followed a moment of unfairly
matched struggle with little grunts of deep effort on her
part, and grim, determined looks on both their faces.

Given Duncan's greater height, weight, and strength,
the outcome of the contest could not be in doubt except
for his indecision. He could not hold her wriggling arms
forever, but if he let her go she would be upon him
tooth and nail. So he held on, and she wrestled.

But the log upon which they fought had had enough.
With a loud crack the end gave way and rolled them
over backwards into the dirt and pine needles.

"Lady Druscilla!" called a voice worriedly. "Where
are you?"

Dru looked at the footman in horror. His wig had
fallen all to one side, and there were smudges of dirt on
his cheek. His eyes were as round as her own.

"It is Lord Sebastian," she whispered in agony.

"Hurry," Duncan said, and struggled to his feet, pulling her up with him. Quickly he plucked pine needles
from her hair and dress. "The handkerchief." She removed it from her pocket and handed it to him. "Er—
moisten it, please." He held it before her mouth, and she
touched it doubtfully with her tongue. He used it to remove a spot on her chin, then returned it.

"Now you look fine enough for a lord," he sneered.

"Do you be quiet," she hissed, and reached very far
up to straighten his wig. She refolded the handkerchief
and held it before his mouth. "Moisten it, please," she
said mockingly, and he complied with a frown. She put
it to a similar use on his cheek.

"Now you look fine enough for a footman," she said,
her lips curling.

"Lady Druscilla?" called Lord Sebastian. He sounded
very much nearer. In a moment they would be found.

"I suppose now I will be sent packing," Duncan
whispered angrily.

She looked at him. She certainly had reason to dismiss him now. Her father could not defend this sort of behavior, no matter what hold the footman had over him. But it would be difficult to explain these last few moments, especially if Duncan were ungentlemanly enough to tell her father *she* had kissed *him*.

She was reluctant for another reason. It would be hard to sack a man who looked as pitiful as this one. There was a jagged tear in his breeches by his right knee, and his cravat was dreadfully stained. A man who couldn't keep his own livery clean would be hard-put to find a position. She didn't want to be responsible for his starving.

With a firm lowering of her eyebrows she whispered, "If you promise—no, *swear* that you will tell no one of this, I will not report your behaviour to my father."

"No one will hear anything from me, of that you can be sure," he snapped.

Dru nodded, took his arm, and began to walk toward the voice. It did seem, she thought heatedly, that he could at least have the grace to be grateful.

"I'm here, Lord Sebastian," she called.

5

It was mid-morning, and several of Lord Cathburn's servants had gathered in the kitchen for bread and cheese and coffee. The earl was a progressive thinker in such matters and had long ago decreed that none of his servants should have to work on an empty stomach.

Martha Freecastle sliced off a healthy slice of pumpernickel and began spreading it with butter from the earl's dairy. "How's Meg doing?" she asked.

Karl Jessup leaned toward her from across the table. Several conversations were going at once in the large kitchen, and it was difficult to hear. "She's ripe as a plum and fit to burst," he answered.

Martha shook her head. "I feel sorry for her, then. But it won't be long now."

"I wisht God would hear you and make it so," Jessup said earnestly.

Jim Jacobs walked over and flung his leg across the bench, cracking his knee on the table in the process. "Garn," he said hopelessly, for such things were always happening to him. He was a thin man without flab or muscle, and his face was asthetically pleasing in the manner of the heavily lidded, beak-nosed subjects painted by the Italian Masters. He'd pushed his wig back to expose a quantity of wiry black-and-grey hair, of which he was unaccountably proud.

"Where's your fine partner?" he asked when the sharpest pain had died away.

"Duncan?" Jessup's eyes clouded. "He don't go in much for thc kitchcn gossip."

"I've noticed that," contributed Pizzy, who sat beside Martha. "My dears, how I wish he would." She raised her eyes heavenward. "What a handsome one he is!"

"Handsome" was a term Jacobs liked only when used to describe himself. "What good is handsome when you consider your own beneath you?" he asked bitterly. "Thinks he's better than us."

"No, he don't," Jessup said. "He's got other things to do, is all."

"Like what?" drawled Jacobs sarcastically.

Like pretending to be one of the Quality at picnics, Jessup thought, *and leaving the woods with the earl's daughter in torn livery and mad as a pike.* But he was too loyal to voice his suspicions and only shrugged.

Thinking now of Lady Druscilla gave him an opportunity to change the subject. "The earl's youngest has smiled at me every day this week. Don't know what this world's coming to."

"Don't I know it!" Pizzy declared happily. "Yesterday I was fixing her hair. You know how I'm always trying to get her to grow her hair long?" She looked at Martha, who nodded sleepily over her breadplate. "That Titus crop she wears is outmoded, but she always says her hair's too curly for anything else. Well. Yesterday I suggests it again, and she says, 'Thank you, Pizzy, I'll consider it.' And she wasn't a bit mad!"

Jacobs nodded and said, "This morning I brought her a delivery from Daley's. Just as I was to hand the package to her, I tripped over a bump in the carpet." The others exchanged knowing looks, which he ignored.

"Anyway, instead of tongue-lashing me, she laughed and said as how that could happen to anyone!"

"Go on!" Martha said, awestruck.

"Things are changing in this house," Jessup said in a wise voice. "You know things are different when Lady Druscilla acts nice."

At that very moment, Dru was listening to her sister play a Haydn sonata. She leaned her head against the chaise lounge's pillows and closed her eyes. The notes sparkled and fell about her like drops of crystal.

Dru had never been happier. For the past week she'd floated on a tide of relief. *It was not her fault; it had never been her fault that Rissa was blind.* Like a litany she repeated the words, and their force never diminished.

Even the scandalous behaviour of the footman could not darken her mood. Duncan had forgotten himself, that was all. She should not have been so accommodating, but he had caught her in a weak moment.

Now it was time to concentrate upon Lord Sebastian. As soon as he made his offer, everything would be settled in the best possible way. Papa could marry his Mrs. Tweetle, and Rissa and she would present no obstacle.

Hopefully Lord Sebastian would kiss her when he asked her to marry him. Now that she'd discovered kisses were so pleasant, she was eager for more. After all, if a kiss from such a one as Duncan could be so pleasing, it was beyond imagining what it would be like with a lord.

The sonata stumbled to a halt. "Oh!" Rissa said angrily. "It is here that I cannot remember. Help me, won't you, Dru?"

Dru bit her lip. "You know I'm not very good at explaining."

"Please try." Rissa was never very patient when it came to her music. "The sonata begins in a B flat, but the Largo movement is in G minor."

Dru went to the shelf and found the Haydn volume. "Oh, Rissa," she moaned. "All of these demisemiquavers! Here are some hemidemisemiquavers as well!"

"But the tempo is very slow, so it does not matter; you do not need to execute them quickly in any case. You know I must hear it slowly." Rissa began to play softly. "The part I need is just after the theme has been stated in G minor, then goes to B flat major. At the point where it diverges from the initial statement, do you see it?"

Dru wanted desperately to help, but the page was a jumbled mass of black and white to her. "Well, I . . ."

"Dru, you cannot remember even the barest rudiments of theory which our music master taught us," she said crossly. "I shall begin it again and you follow along until I reach the part in question."

Dru swallowed. Rissa was more than ordinarily tense about her practicing today. In fact, she had seemed increasingly irritable since the picnic, and Dru could not understand it. It was almost as if one of them must be prickly, and that as her own happiness increased, Rissa's decreased proportionately.

To her vast relief, Hayes appeared at that moment in the doorway. "There is a visitor in the library," he announced.

"Lord Sebastian?" Dru asked eagerly.

"Mr. James Burke," corrected Hayes.

"Oh." Dru looked at Rissa, whose face wore a little frown. "Papa is still not at home?"

"No, Lady Druscilla."

Dru wondered if Burke had come to see her. She knew that, other than a carriage ride, it was improper to see a gentleman alone unless he had obtained permission to pay his addresses. But Hayes had not said Mr. Burke called only on herself. Doubtless he wanted to see her sister as much as he did her, if not more.

"Shall we see him, Rissa?"

"Of course. Why don't you show him into the music room, Hayes."

James Burke entered a moment later. His appearance was faultlessly conservative. He wore a black morning coat with broad lapels over a stiff white shirt and pantaloons. Dru was glad to note his collar was not overhigh; such had been the style in London last year, and she had thought it ridiculous.

They greeted him politely, and he sat down. "I apologize, Lady Druscilla, for not calling earlier," he said, an expression of sincerity in his large eyes. "I wished to visit immediately after the Winters's dinner, but business concerns called me away."

When Dru thanked him, he added, "I was sorry to hear you were unwell that evening, Lady Clarissa. But it is good to to see you are recovered."

Rissa inclined her head but said nothing. *Her mind is still on that horrible Haydn,* Dru thought, forgetting she had delighted in the music until called upon to read it.

When the silence lengthened, Dru said, "I never did ask you about your year in America, Mr. Burke. Did you enjoy your stay there?"

He laughed briefly. "I don't think 'enjoy' is quite the correct word. And please call me James. We have known one another all our lives, after all."

But only slightly, Dru reflected. Their mothers had been passing friends, but when his mother died ten years before, the connection was broken. Moreover, he was more than twelve years their senior and had always seemed remote until his brief courtship of Rissa.

Unwilling to disagree, she said, "Then perhaps you will give us your impressions of America, James. Were the Americans hostile toward you, so soon after the war?"

"Even though the ink is hardly dry on the Treaty of Ghent, I was courted by the leading citizens of New York," he said with a wry smile. "I daresay they'd sell their souls for an English accent. But it's because they have no sense of society, no aristocracy. Just a jumble of merchants and bankers, doctors and lawyers attempting to form some sort of hierarchy. They may preach democracy, but in their hearts they long for royalty."

If that is so, Dru wondered, *then why did they fight so viciously to rid themselves of it forty years before?*

"We always strive for the unattainable," he elaborated. "It's a part of our nature."

Dru could not help wondering if he spoke of his pursuit of Rissa. She watched him closely, but he cast no yearning glances in her sister's direction. In point of fact, he seemed eminently correct; his manner and voice were more polite than any gentleman of her acquaintance. Mayhap it stemmed from being brought up by a widowed mother.

"Were you in America on business or pleasure?" Rissa asked.

"Business, my lady. I've heard so much of the opportunities there, I wanted to see for myself. I was fortunate enough to find several hundred acres along the Georgia coast. It's prime farmland, especially for cotton."

"You won't be leaving us soon, will you?"

"I've no plans for the immediate future, Lady Druscilla. There are many preparations to be made, and I'm in no hurry. I've not entirely decided to emigrate anyway; many such plantations are run by proxy, if one is fortunate enough to find a competent steward."

Dru immediately thought of reports of brutal slavery

on such plantations and shuddered. If James noticed her distaste, he gave no sign.

Hayes entered bearing a tray of lemonade, but the gentleman rose. "Thank you, but I shall not stay for refreshment. I wanted only to pay my respects, and also to offer myself as escort if you attend the musicale at the Winters's on tomorrow evening."

"Oh, I'm sorry," Dru said. "My father and Lord Sebastian accompany us."

There was a slight stiffening in his manner. "I see. Perhaps another time, then."

"There is no reason he should not accompany us as well," said Rissa.

As Dru rushed to agree, James interrupted, saying, "Thank you, no; there is no point in overcrowding the carriage. I will see you there."

"We are having Sebastian over for dinner on the evening following the musicale," Rissa said kindly. "Perhaps you would join us then?"

"Thank you, Lady Clarissa, Lady Druscilla," he said, bowing. "I should be delighted."

As they rose to curtsey, Dru noted the fond light in his eyes as he looked at Rissa; there was, beyond all doubting, a look of hope there. Feeling her observation, he turned the same expression toward her. The smile he wore greatly animated his somber, handsome features.

When he departed, Rissa asked to be taken to her room. Dru was grateful to be delivered from deciphering the sonata, but she expressed her fear that Rissa might have another of her headaches.

"No, I'm fine," Rissa replied. "Just a little weary."

"I hope James didn't tire you," Dru said as they entered the hall.

She couldn't resist stealing a glance at Duncan as they passed the footmen. Other than a slight tensing of his jaw, Duncan in no way acknowledged her presence.

For one absurd moment she was mightily tempted to chuck him under the chin or poke a finger at his ribs. Or stand before him with her eyes crossed. What would he do then? But she fought the impulse and led Rissa toward the stairs.

"It was good of you to invite him to dinner," Dru continued. "He seemed very disappointed about tomorrow evening. I think he still has an attachment for you, Rissa. I don't suppose you would reconsider . . . ?"

"No," she said firmly. In a softer voice she added, "No, I don't think I could, although James is a very sweet man. Perhaps too sweet, too perfect. More than any one thing, that is why I rejected his suit."

Dru pulled her aside while a maid, her arms full of bedding, passed by them in the upstairs corridor. "He was too perfect?" she asked incredulously. "I didn't know such a man existed."

"Now, Dru," Rissa said with a shaky smile. "What of your Lord Sebastian?"

"I agree that he is close to ideal. But he is a trifle class-conscious, have you noticed?"

Rissa looked surprised. "You are not accusing him of snobbery, are you, Dru? But I thought you felt . . ."

"I know I've been guilty of it myself in the past," Dru said self-consciously, "but I am trying not to be." Suddenly she thought virtuously, *Duncan should hear me!* And then: *No, he shouldn't; he might think he'd influenced on earl's daughter.*

"Well, it seems a minor flaw to me," said Rissa. "I'm sure with the guidance of an enlightened wife, he will soon lose even that minor defect."

They entered Rissa's bedroom, and she walked to her bed, stacked several pillows atop one another, and lay down. Dru sat on the edge of the bed and said, "But about James. Why would you reject a perfect man?"

A line appeared in Rissa's forehead as she thought.

"It is almost as though there is nothing there, Dru; nothing behind his genteel ways. He would never disagree with anything I said; he always did the expected thing. The only time he showed any real emotion was when I rejected his suit. He became angry and wanted to know if I would have spurned him did he have a title. And you know that does not matter to me."

Dru acknowledged the truth of this. "It just seems a shame," she added. "It isn't right that the younger should be the first of our generation to wear the tiara."

Rissa knew she referred to the Selby Tiara, a priceless, diamond-encrusted heirloom bestowed by Queen Anne to an ancestor for heroism at Blenheim. The tiara was traditionally worn by the inheriting earl's daughters on their wedding day. Or by his sons' brides.

"Of course it is right, if circumstances lead that way," Rissa said crisply. "You shall be the first to wear it, and I do not mind. Lord Sebastian will be overcome with your beauty."

"Well," Dru said, a soft smile playing about her lips, "he has not asked me yet."

"He will soon, I am sure of it," Rissa replied. "And now, dear, I should like to sleep."

"Of course!" Dru hurriedly removed herself from the bed. "I will see you at luncheon."

When she heard the door close, Rissa rose from the bed and felt for the bell pull. Martha had better come soon. She had not wanted to tell Dru, but one of her headaches was coming on, and from the feel of the gathering thunderclouds in her skull, it was going to be a devil.

By the following evening, Rissa had recovered sufficiently to attend the Winters's musicale. It was a tight squeeze within the earl's carriage, but Lord Sebastian was happy to have taken the extra time to offer his escort to the Selby sisters. It would mean an additional return trip to the Winters's late at night, but time spent in the young ladies' presence was well worth it.

Not to mention it meant fewer moments at Harry's house, a place that had grown uncomfortable since the arrival of Mason and Charity Trentley. Though to be fair, the situation was not as warm as he thought it would be. He'd not seen the couple since their wedding, or rather, their second wedding, their first being a Gretna Green affair. At the time of their public joining, the sight of his best friend and first love's union had pierced him at every turn.

He'd expected similar feelings at Harry's. But when he first set eyes on Charity last evening, he discovered the pain had dulled to an ache, like the healing of an old wound.

Mayhaps Charity had been correct after all. When he'd asked for her hand in marriage months ago, she had let him down as easily as possible, saying that one day he'd discover a young lady more deserving of his love than herself. Well, he didn't know about the "more deserving" part, but perhaps his association with the young ladies *had* eased the soreness in his heart.

Lady Dru and Lady Rissa. They sat across from him in the carriage, with Mrs. Tweetle beside them. The three of them were discussing the evening's entertainment. The evening was chilly, and Lady Dru wore a green velvet pelisse which deepened the colour of her eyes. Lady Rissa's cloak was black and trimmed in swan's down, a startling contrast against her fairness.

Both of them were beautiful in their own way. And both possessed great quantities of character: Lady Dru, so spirited and devoted to her sister; Lady Rissa, the most valiant and compelling creature he'd ever known.

She had a way about her that made him feel extraordinary, and she didn't even know what he looked like!

This meant a very great deal to a man who had known women to swoon at the sight of him. Surely it meant she liked him for *himself.*

Back and forth his eyes went between them. Back and forth.

Lord Sebastian was not given to introspection, so it was only now coming to him that he was a man in trouble. Very great trouble indeed.

He was glad to feel the coach pull to a stop. Lord Cathburn leaned his head out the window and said cheerfully, "Looks to be a frightful crush."

They were fifth in a line of carriages depositing guests. The sensible thing might have been to disembark and walk the few remaining feet to the manor house, but all knew such haste would appear overeager, so they awaited their turn.

Dru descended from the carriage with the help of the omnipresent Duncan. She looked at him, but he turned his face impassively to assist Rissa. *What will he do now?* Dru wondered. *Will he play dice with the other servants? Chase rabbits? If he could go inside, would he entrance the guests with tales of Scottish ghosts?*

Lord Sebastian gave an arm to each lady and led them into the house. Inside, the butler accepted cloaks and reticules and hats and handed them to one of two alternating maids for safekeeping.

The Winters had formed a receiving line with their honoured guests and were introducing them to each party as they entered. Dru was startled by the attractiveness of the two musicians. When introduced to the Earl of Ashbury's son, she felt a little shiver of delight at the darkness of his eyes and hair and his expression of warm interest when he looked at her. But when he turned to his wife, his eyes were scorching and tender upon her all at once, and Dru knew a moment's longing. To have a gentleman look upon her in such a way would surely make her knees weak.

Yet Lady Charity returned his glance with one of equal intensity and did not seem a bit overwhelmed. But she was so devastating; her hair was as dark as his, though her eyes were a deep blue, and she radiated charm and self-assurance; she'd probably had to deal with such looks from men all her life, and it was nothing to her.

The couple was dressed in black and white, the colours of musicians and mourners. Lord Mason's waistcoat was trimmed in red piping, and Charity wore a red velvet ribbon in her hair.

Dru passed through the line feeling insipid and colourless. She wished for Lord Sebastian to look at her with dark, smoldering eyes. She longed to feel that way about him. She wanted to have shining black hair that glowed in the candlelight.

When they had finished greeting their hosts, Lord Sebastian and his two ladies drifted into the front parlour and found seats. While the viscount went to search for refreshments, the earl and Mrs. Tweetle wandered off to find a less crowded room.

"Mrs. Tweetle seemed unusually talkative this evening," Rissa said. "I think she grows more comfortable with us." She tilted her head. "Perhaps it was because you were so gracious, Dru."

Dru murmured noncommitally. She didn't want to dismay her sister by telling her what an effort it had been.

Rissa looked elegant in her pink-spotted sarsenet gown. Her hair was caught up in curls intertwined amidst a bandeau of pink satin rosebuds. The colour brought out the pale pink of her cheeks, and her eyes sparkled.

Dru was relieved that Rissa seemed set to enjoy the

evening. Since her blindness, large gatherings sometimes distressed her.

"I believe everyone in two counties is here, Rissa," Dru said, and began to tell her the names of people she knew. "Oh dear," she whispered after a moment, "here are the Petersham girls, who have wandered past this room four times. They are beyond a doubt following Lord Sebastian, for he is coming now with cups of punch."

Looking slightly harried, the viscount served the ladies and sat down, only to pop up again when Claudia and Ceile approached.

"Oh, hello," Claudia said in a very affected voice. She swung her fan up to her face with the precision of one drawing a weapon. With a snap of her wrist she flung it open to curtain the lower regions of her face, an action that caused Lord Sebastian to flinch in order to avoid being struck.

Realizing her error, Claudia began to flutter the fan furiously, but obviously didn't know whether to apologize or ignore the incident. Her eyes rolled in her head as one possessed.

Fish eyes, Dru thought maliciously. *And there she stands without allowing the viscount to reseat himself, and here we sit, subjected to looking up into her doughy face.* At least Ceile, who would have been pretty except for the fact that her flame-red hair and eyelashes gave her a woefully naked and wistful look, had the social sense to look ashamed.

Claudia smacked her lips together and took a deep breath. "Pretty evening, hisn't it?"

The viscount looked about him for a window and said that it was indeed.

Claudia gave a wild trill of laughter. "Ooh, my lord, you are so witty!" She snapped her fan shut and tapped his arm with it. Leaning forward as though imparting secrets, she added, "We don't get many such fine London wits around here. Nor many who looks as fine as you."

Keeping his eyes on the fan, Lord Sebastian thanked her.

"Not *any* who looks as fine as you do, to be truthful," she said, giving him a coquettish stare. "Hisn't that right, Ceile?" When no answer seemed forthcoming, she turned angrily to her sister and yanked on her arm. "Hisn't that right?" she repeated.

"What?" Ceile removed her gaze from her shoes to look at Claudia. "Oh! Yes."

The vicar's elder daughter looked at the viscount and shrugged as if to say, *What can one do with such a sister?*

And then her eyes became adoring again, and she opened her mouth to speak, but inspiration did not strike her anew. After a long moment of standing with open mouth and searching eyes, she turned on Ceile with renewed vehemence and said, "Well, go on, you biscuit-head! You know we must find Father before the program begins."

When they departed, the viscount sat down with a sigh of relief.

"Miss Petersham has a voice that slides up and down like a pennywhistle," Rissa said solemnly.

"Rissa!" Dru giggled in delighted shock.

"It is only an observation," Rissa said, trying not to smile.

"And here is another," Sebastian said, grinning. "Everyone seems to be gathering for the entertainment."

They placed their cups on the table and walked toward the saloon. Just as they entered the room, Dru heard a wavery voice calling her name from the midst of the crowd.

"There you are! There you are, Lady Druscilla!"

"It is Miss Lumquist," Dru said softly, and turned to acknowledge her. The viscount guided them near the wall and away from the tide of music lovers flowing toward their seats.

All that could be seen of Miss Lumquist was a fluttering hand waving a handkerchief above the shoulders of the crowd, but gradually the old woman worked her way to them. She was dressed in a long-sleeved gown of brown wool. Dru wondered how she bore the heat, but only her hair seemed bothered, wisping away from its clasp as it did, like molting feathers.

"I've had a vision, Lady Druscilla," Miss Lumquist said, and stepped very closely to her. As her voice was overloud and her breath unpleasant, Dru leaned into the wall as far as she was able. "A vision . . . about you."

Dru felt a little chill. She didn't believe in such things, but Miss Lumquist *had* predicted Harry's marriage, and she *did* find a missing reticule at an altar guild meeting at church. Such things might be explained away, but it was hard to ignore the zealous light in her eyes.

They were attracting attention, perhaps because Miss Lumquist was weaving from side to side and moaning. Dru glanced at the viscount in embarrassment, but he seemed amused, while Rissa looked puzzled.

The old lady stopped chanting with a suddenness that reclaimed Dru's attention. "Beware!" the woman shouted, and raised her arm heavenward. Her faded eyes fastened Dru to the wall like a basilisk.

To the young lady's mortification, the entire room fell silent in witness of this pre-recital drama. Miss Lumquist closed her eyes and began to sway again. "Beware the water, the deep, deep water," she sang.

"Y-yes, ma'am, I shall," Dru said, and tried to move away. As her arm was linked in Lord Sebastian's, she unceremoniously dragged him and Rissa with her.

They had almost made their escape when the querulous voice called after her again. Dru turned reluctantly to see a trembling finger pointing in her direction.

"And most of all," Miss Lumquist shouted, "most of all, BEWARE THE BROWN-HAIRED MAN!"

Dru nodded quickly and pulled the others into a row near the back of the room. She pressed her hands to her hot cheeks and tried to stop trembling.

Lord Sebastian saw her discomfort and whispered jokingly, "Well, I'm glad you don't have to beware me, since my hair is not brown."

She gave him a tremulous smile and stared at her hands.

Duncan was a brown-haired man. And hadn't she always had a bad feeling about him?

6

Harry approached the stage area. He, too, seemed shaken by Miss Lumquist's outburst, for he stumbled and blustered his way through the introduction. But perhaps it was only his natural shyness.

And then Lord Mason began to play his guitar. Dru felt her concerns and suspicions drift away. He was a magician weaving a spell of gossamer sounds, teasing her with tastes of Spain and Italy and England.

The guitar was only just becoming known in England, having been imported from Spain by soldiers stationed in the Peninsula. Dru had never heard one played before, and she was entranced.

Peering past Lord Sebastian, Dru noted that Rissa was equally moved. But it was Lady Charity's performance on the pianoforte that stirred her sister to tears. After performing an ambitious Beethoven sonata, the musician concluded with a composition of her brother's, a piece so rich in harmony, so soaring in melody, that Rissa sprang to her feet when the applause began. Others followed suit, so that Lady Charity was forced to bow again and again, a blush of pleasure on her cheeks.

The last selection was to be sung by Lord Mason and accompanied by his wife. When he returned to the stage after her wild reception, he looked ruefully at the audience and said, "I don't know if I dare follow my wife's performance!" When several encouraging shouts were heard, he laughed. "Very well, then. I'd like to sing a ballad written last year by a young composer named Franz Schubert. In English, it is called 'The Erlking,' and is based upon Goethe's poem."

He began to sing. Dru was spellbound as the story of the wild horseride unfolded: the frightened child in the arms of his father; the seductive, deadly power of the Erlking as he claims the boy for his own. The accompaniment on the pianoforte suggested the frantic pace of pounding hooves; Lord Mason's voice captured the haunting drama of the melody.

When they finished, the listeners rose as one, shouting and clapping their appreciation.

"Take me to Lady Charity," Rissa begged. "I must speak with her."

Dru looked at the crush of people surrounding the performers and said, "I don't think we can just now. But remember, we are invited to supper; you can speak with her then."

Rissa looked so disappointed that Sebastian was moved to say, "I'll escort her to Charity, Lady Dru. Why don't you await us in the parlour?"

Dru looked toward the stage area again. It seemed the entire room stood in line to shower the couple with compliments. She had no desire for such a long wait, and besides, Miss Lumquist was in that line. Dru agreed to the viscount's plan.

To her dismay, Cedric Bottomsby and his mother had had the same notion and walked a few paces before her in the hall. Fortunately they were leaving, for they requested the butler to bring their coats. Since she did not wish to speak to them, Dru dashed into a small receiving room and leaned out carefully to watch their departure.

Cedric waited impatiently, his foot tapping a staccato pattern on the wooden floor. His gaze was fixed upon a portrait of one of Harry's ancestors.

Mrs. Bottomsby's head turned this way and that as she examined the Winters's furnishings with hard, beady eyes. She seemed particularly taken with a Chinese vase sitting upon a Sheraton table near the front door. After giving a cursory glance toward the cloak room, she went to the table and lifted the vase to examine its bottom, dislodging its contents as she did so.

The butler emerged at that moment. Though one long eyebrow lifted eloquently, any emotion that he felt at seeing the rose-and-water-strewn floor was masked by long experience with the incomprehensible ways of the gentry.

" 'Twas falling over," said Cedric's mother in her flat, nasal voice. "Saved the pitcher, I did."

The butler accepted the proffered vase. "Thank you, madame," he said austerely. "Your coats."

A servant emerged bearing the Bottomsby's outer garments, and Dru's eyes widened in disbelief.

The servant was Duncan.

Her amazement was so great that she almost divulged her hiding place, but she contained herself long enough for the Bottomsbys to leave. As soon as the door closed behind them, she hurried past the startled butler and entered the cloak room.

Duncan had his back turned and was quietly searching the pockets of a gentleman's grey woolen overcoat.

"Duncan!" she whispered in shock. "What are you doing?"

He turned immediately and dropped the coat. "Hello, Lady Druscilla," he said. Colour flooded his cheeks. "I hope you enjoyed the musicale."

She walked closer and glared at him. He looked toward the door as though he wished to bolt from the room.

"I asked you a question, Duncan."

"Did you? Oh, yes. What am I doing. Well, I was bored, waiting outside, and I offered my services to Mr. Briggs over there. He said the maids would be glad of the break, so here I am. Since your family won't be needing the carriage for a long while, I thought it would be all right."

"That was very commendable of you, Duncan," she said evenly. "Most thoughtful." She moved casually to the side and plucked at the grey overcoat. "I suppose you meant to be helpful to the guests as well, by cleaning their pockets of unnecessary . . . items. Like pocket change, for example?"

"Oh no, milady. You thought I was—" He gave a strained laugh. "No. I was merely checking the coat labels. Mr. Briggs has his maids place the name of the owner on a piece of paper and insert it in a pocket. I was trying to familiarize myself with each name, so that guests will not have to wait overlong for their wraps."

There was a long pause as Dru continued to nail him with her eyes, debating. Duncan met her gaze bravely, a portrait of injured honesty.

"Oh," she said, deflating. "Very well, then, Duncan. Carry on." At the doorway she gave him one final glance of suspicion, raised her chin, and walked away with great dignity.

Duncan expelled a large breath and sat down among the pelisses and cloaks and shawls. He opened his hand and smoothed the crumpled edges of the paper he'd found. It was an order for lumber, from the looks of it. He examined it carefully, shook his head, and replaced it in the pocket of the grey coat.

He stared dismally at the remaining pockets surrounding him and rubbed the bridge of his nose. Then he looked at the doorway as though expecting a petite figure in lavendar to appear.

"Druscilla Selby, you miss very little," he said quietly. And began to laugh.

After the other guests departed, the small party remaining gathered in the front parlour to await supper. James Burke had joined Lord Cathburn and his family as the only non-resident guests invited to remain.

"Your brother Stephen is a formidable talent," Rissa said to Charity. "And to think he is so young! I should like to try to play the piece he wrote."

"It will soon be published, and I shall send you a copy. Although . . ." Charity looked distressed.

Rissa smiled. "Don't be troubled. Dru will play it for me slowly, and I shall learn it in that way."

Dear Lord, Dru thought miserably.

"It's unfortunate there is not some method for reading through one's sense of touch," said James.

"But there is," Lord Mason commented. "Charity and I have just returned from our wedding trip, which was delayed by several circumstances." He looked at her fondly. "We visited Paris, since that ancient city is now available to us once more. There we heard of a school for blind children which was established by Valentin . . ."

"Haüy," Charity supplied.

"Yes. He taught the children to read by embossing letters upon paper."

"I have heard of it," Rissa said. "Such a school now exists in Liverpool as well. It's just unfortunate there is so little printed in this manner. And doubly unfortunate that music cannot be learned in this way."

"But what of Maria Theresia von Paradis, Lady Clarrisa?" Charity asked. "Have you heard of her?"

Rissa admitted she had not.

"She is a blind composer and pianist from Vienna. A clever invention was made for her, a composition board, upon which she notates her compositions. She studied with Salieri and Righini and toured triumphantly in Paris and London as well as Austria during the last century. She is older now and does not tour as much, but a few years ago she formed an institute for music education. The reason I know about her is because she is so celebrated in Vienna, where my brother studies. It is said she performs sixty concertos from memory, and that both Mozart and Salieri wrote compositions for her."

"How inspiring," Rissa said weakly.

"Was she blind from birth?" asked Mrs. Tweetle.

"I believe she became blind as a child," Charity answered. "And there was a brief period when some sight was restored to her by the magnetist, Mesmer."

"I thought Mesmer was a charlatan and a fraud!" Dru exclaimed.

"So some said. But mesmerism is a fascinating idea, do you not think? And it did seem to work for Madame Paradis, however briefly."

"I wonder . . ." Rissa breathed, her eyes shining with hope.

"Don't go thinking it, dearest," Lord Cathburn said. "The fellow died last year. I recall reading it in the papers."

James's voice became entreating. "Surely he had followers. Someone must be carrying on his work."

"I don't know." Charity bit her lip thoughtfully. "But he died in Baden. Perhaps if one inquired there . . . but I don't wish to raise false hopes, Lady Clarissa. I suspect most forms of blindness cannot be reversed by any means."

"I shall be happy to dispatch some letters straightaway," Sebastian declared. "Nothing can be gained by speculation."

James turned his large, gentle eyes toward Sebastian. "Baden is near Vienna, is it not? I have friends in Vienna. I will inquire as well."

The viscount stared at him. "Good," he said.

"Excellent," James returned.

Charity watched them both, then looked at Rissa, whose face registered a mixture of hope and doubt. She saw Dru leave Sebastian's side to press her sister's hand.

Oh dear, she thought.

"Do you stay awhile?" Lord Cathburn asked. "We'd like to have you to dinner."

"Our visit is woefully brief," said Lord Mason. "We're journeying on tomorrow, since there are many responsibilities awaiting us."

"Charity's father is recovering from an attack of apoplexy," Cynthia explained.

Lord Mason nodded. "And my father and Cynthia's mother are expecting a blessed event within a few months."

Lord Cathburn's eyes grew round. "Your father—and Cynthia's mother—"

"Well, they are married to one another," Harry said, embarrassed. "They have been for years."

"Didn't mean that, my boy! I knew they was married." He gave Mrs. Tweetle a blinding grin. "Getting a bit long in the tooth, ain't they? For little ones, I mean?"

Lord Mason smiled. "Not too long, evidently."

Dru stared at her father in annoyance. And then Briggs announced supper, and she took Sebastian's free arm in relief. Surely at table she would be spared further expressions of inappropriate masculine pride.

* * *

Some hours later, the viscount returned from escorting the earl's daughters home. The Winters's house was dark but for the lamps lit outside the door and a faint illumination in the front parlour. Briggs opened the door for him and locked it, then nodded toward the parlour.

"Lady Charity awaits you," he said softly, and drifted away.

Sebastian's heart began to pound. What must the butler think? What could be in Charity's mind?

Charity laughed softly and went to kiss his cheek. "Do not look so guilty, you big silly. Mason knows I am here."

"Oh," he said, vastly relieved. And then, "You are looking exceptionally well. You are still the most lovely lady I know."

"Do you mean four months of married life have not yet ruined me?" she teased. "I believe you flatter me, now that you know I am safe."

"No, truly. You wear happiness like a garment. It suits you." And thought: *What would it be to bring such happiness to another? Would that I could have brought it to you.*

As though reading his mind, she said, "It is Mason who suits me." She tilted her head and looked at him speculatively. "Just as I believe you have found someone who suits you."

He swallowed. "I?"

"You can't deny it, Sebastian. I have seen that special look in your eye when you look at Lady Clarissa."

"Lady Rissa!" he exclaimed. "Surely you mean Lady Dru." But his heart denied the words as soon as they were said.

She nodded. "It is as I thought. I saw you escorting the two of them this evening. They are both beautiful and worthy young ladies, but I sensed your confusion.

You'd best sort it out soon, Bastian, or you will leave a broken heart."

He gave her a look of dread. "You don't think that—that both of their affections are engaged, do you?"

She gave him a wry look. "It would be hard to avoid, dear. You are not easy to resist."

"I began by calling on Lady Dru," he said solemnly. "Rissa simply became a part of our outings. Charity, I cannot stop thinking of her. And yet, she is . . ."

"She is blind," the lady supplied.

He looked at his boot tops. "Yes."

"And Lord Montgomery has a liking for perfection, does he not?" she asked gently.

He turned away from her and sat in a chair, leaning his elbows on his knees. He rubbed his temples dejectedly.

Charity knelt beside the chair and looked at him with compassion. "My dear," she whispered, "no one is perfect."

He gave her a tender smile. "You are."

"I encourage you to speak with Mason about that. He'll inform you otherwise." She rose to her feet and touched his shoulder. "Pray do not let this need rob you of all joy. When love comes to you, it is a precious gift. Do not deny it."

She gave his shoulder a gentle squeeze and slipped from the room.

For a long while, Sebastian stayed behind in the dimly lit parlour. When he finally ascended the stairs, the candle had diminished itself to a sputtering flame.

Dru stared out the window as Hayes served her breakfast plate. After a night of restless thoughts, she felt as animated as the reclining shepherdess on the mantel. Rissa seemed in poor spirits, too. But their father was almost offensively boisterous and hearty in his manner.

"Mrs. Tweetle and I are going on an excursion today to Corfe Castle," he explained, when Dru asked the reason for his joviality. "Can it be believed? She's never seen it.'

"Does she understand there are only ruins, Papa?"

" 'Tis not the castle walls that are important, Clarissa," he said. "Think of the history of the place. King Edward was murdered there by his stepmother. Lady Bankes defended it during the civil dispute." He forked a large bite of kipper into his mouth and chewed. "Anyway, when we're done with that, I thought I'd take her by the clayworks, maybe find a dish for her collection."

"It sounds a very full day," Dru said languidly, and poked at her eggs.

"Yes, it shall be." He took a final bite of steak, wiped his mouth with the napkin, and pushed back his chair. Sighing pleasurably, he walked to the window and looked out. The gardeners were busily clipping and trimming the hedges. The green, smooth grass stretched in all directions from the house until it met the road and wood.

Green, not red, should be the colour of the carpet unfurled for royalty, he thought. *Exactly this shade of green. Such is the colour of life, for an Englishman.*

Dru placed her fork beside her plate and looked at him curiously. "What are you thinking about, Papa?" she asked.

He turned from the window. She noted the way the sun highlighted the pink of his scalp through his sparse hair. In the library was a portrait of her mother and father painted just after their wedding trip. The earl's hair had been thick and full, his face thin, tautly muscled, and unlined.

Her spirits sank a little lower.

Lord Cathburn seemed to absorb her mood, for his merry eyes grew solemn. "It's just passed my mind," he said, nodding toward the portrait over the sideboard of a handsome young man, "how differently things could have turned out had Edmond survived."

"Would we have lived in want, Papa?" Rissa asked.

He chuckled. "Hardly that. Probably would have resided at the estate in Sussex." Life would have been simpler, too, had his elder brother lived. Less responsibility, if less luxury. *And maybe,* he thought with a pang, *maybe my daughter would not be living her days in darkness.*

"It would have been very different not being an earl's daughter," Dru commented.

"Well," he said expansively and patted his stomach, 'tis not a thing you need dwell upon, for Edmond played fast and loose and got himself shot for it. So here we are. And though I was that fond of him, he brought it on himself. Had the pick of all the lovelies in three shires, he did, and still had an eye for the forbidden. Every young man of sense should know not to cross a jealous husband."

Realizing the subject was not the most appropriate for his maiden daughters, he cleared his throat in embarrassment and walked toward the door, saying gruffly he'd best be getting ready for his outing with Mrs. Tweetle.

When he had gone, Rissa asked, "What time does Lord Sebastian come for our ride?"

"At one."

"Since he will be staying for dinner, and James comes as well, I think I should like to lie down until luncheon. I didn't sleep well last night."

Dru expressed her desire to do the same, and the young ladies repaired to their bedchambers.

Pizzy was in the process of making her bed, and Dru

dismissed her, telling her to take the rest of the morning off. Pizzy's eyes were glowing with amazed gratitude when she left.

Dru fell upon the half-made bed and buried her face in the pillow. She longed to be able to stop her wandering thoughts as easily as she hid her eyes from the sight of this room.

She could not stop thinking about Duncan.

The previous evening had been interesting in many ways, particularly the conversation with Lady Charity concerning mesmerism. What if Rissa could have her sight restored? How joyful they all would be; so joyful that surely nothing could make them sad again.

But instead of finding her thoughts occupied by hope, Duncan's image dominated her mind. He was like an interloper pushing his way into her previously well-ordered brain. She clenched her fists, she pounded the bedding, but nothing could drive him out.

Images of Duncan haunted her. His golden eyes, sometimes serious and compassionate, but often teasing; the tallness of him and his strong, masculine presence; the traces of gentleness and warmth beneath a servantly facade; the soft touch of his lips hinting at deeper fires fiercely restrained.

Other Duncans marched behind her eyelids. Duncan, spying upon her and the viscount from the bushes—the rabbit had been a ruse, she was certain now, with a terrible sinking of her heart.

Duncan, giving orders to the groomsmen.

Duncan, searching the pockets of the Winter's guests. He'd not been there to relieve the unknown maids from their duty, she knew that; she was no fool. She had let it go last night, wanting to believe. But in the light of day it was impossible to deny the mounting evidence of secretiveness and subterfuge.

What is he about? she asked herself, tears of frustration and dismay beginning to spill from her tightly clenched eyes. *It cannot be good.*

Her father would not listen to her suspicions; she knew that much by now. And Rissa was too fragile to be troubled unnecessarily. Besides, she was too fond of the footman and would probably laugh. He had forever endeared himself by restoring Satin to her.

Dru lifted her head from the pillow. *Rissa* . . . Could she be his plan? Was he a fortune-hunter hoping to ensnare the affection of a lonely blind girl who happened to be one of the wealthiest young ladies in England? But that didn't explain the new servants and their deference to him . . .

It was exasperating that only Miss Lumquist, of all people, had put voice to her own suspicions. *Beware the brown-haired man,* indeed. She had known something was wrong from the moment she laid eyes upon him.

However, it seemed anything she learned about him would have to be discovered on her own.

Coming to a decision, Dru sat up and splashed her face with water from the basin. She started to tug on the bell pull, but remembered Pizzy would be counting on her morning off, and went to find Hayes herself.

He was in the pantry when she found him, supervising the polishing of one of their silver tea sets. Jim Jacobs appeared to be finding the task distasteful, she noted, and looked grateful for the interruption.

"Who is scheduled to accompany our ride today, Hayes?" she asked.

"Duncan, my lady," he replied. "He normally assists Lady Rissa in her riding." He looked surprised, as though she should have known that.

She did, but wanted his reassurance. Now she could put her plan into motion without impediment.

* * *

Lord Sebastian's eyes were tender as he watched Rissa descend the stairs on the arm of her maid. The young lady was looking incomparably fine in her plum-coloured riding habit. One of the sewing maids had concocted a divided skirt to make easier her riding astride; but she had done it cleverly, cutting the material so full that it appeared in no way unusual.

"Where is Lady Dru?" asked the viscount.

"She has a headache and has cried off this afternoon. And though I offered to stay, she begged that we go ahead with our outing."

"I'm sorry she's not feeling well," Sebastian commiserated, but his eyes were joyful as he looked upon her.

Dru watched the three of them ride away from the window of one of the guest rooms. Duncan's hair had gleamed almost red in the sunlight as he held Rissa.

But she could not think about that now.

She stared at the keys in her hand and tossed them nervously. It had been difficult getting those keys. The servants had looked up from their meal in surprise. They did not often see her enter the kitchens twice in one day. It was fortunate they could not see into the butler's pantry from the table, for every eye was upon her as she entered it.

Naturally, it was her right to seize any key to any room in the house at any time. But she didn't want the servants to fear she would invade their privacy. And they mustn't know there was only one room she was interested in.

It was time to move, now, while most of the servants lingered over their luncheon. She didn't want anyone to see her entering Duncan's room and telling him about it.

The only stair to the attic rooms was the servant's back stair. When she ascended it, she was struck by the narrow height of the ceiling in the servant's hall, the small width of the corridor, the musty smell of moth-damaged carpet, and the overwhelming heat. She'd not been up here since she was a child, back in the days when she and Rissa played hide-and-seek all over the vast regions of their home.

My goodness, she thought, *their quarters could so easily be made more pleasant. Papa must be informed.*

The men's chambers were nearest the stair, she recalled. And then looked in dismay at the double row of doors. How was she to know which room was Duncan's? The key ring had been on a peg labeled "Servants' Rooms," but, other than room numbers on each key, there were no further designations. There seemed nothing for it but to enter each chamber in turn and hope for something of a personal nature that would identify the room's owner.

Condemning herself as a noodle-brain for thinking she could accomplish her task before the servants began filtering upstairs, she knocked at the first door. When no answer was heard, she pressed a key into the lock and turned the knob.

"My goodness," she repeated to herself.

The room was only large enough to contain a single bed, a table with washbasin, a large, heavy wardrobe, and a straight-backed wooden chair. There was no carpet, and the floor was of rough, unvarnished wood. Water stains marked the ceiling in several places, and the walls had not seen paint in a very long time.

Does Papa know about this? she wondered. *How can the servants live in such surroundings? After a hard day of labour, to have only this to come home to. . . .*

But the room was clean, thanks no doubt to the maids assigned to the servants' wing. And she could spare no more time regretting the workers' lack of amenities; that could be dealt with later. Feeling like the trespasser she was, she went to the wardrobe and opened it.

A spare suit of livery hung within, along with a pair

of rough trousers and a coarsely woven shirt. Workman's boots, woolen socks, and undergarments lay at the bottom.

She felt a moment's discouragement. With no more personal items than this, how could she hope to identify Duncan's room? And then she thought, *Of course! Duncan's livery will be larger.*

Since this livery was only for an average-sized man, Dru re-locked the door and moved swiftly to the one across the hall. Room after room she entered, moving directly to the wardrobes. Since she now knew how to look, no more than a moment was spent in each room. Still, time was passing swiftly, and the thought was growing that she would *never* find Duncan's chamber.

But at last she came upon an eighteenth-century uniform so long that the kneepants had been folded twice over the hanger. Eagerly she ran her hands along the bottom of the wardrobe, disturbing the few garments that lay there. She felt inside pockets, even turned his boots upside down.

Dru could not say what she looked for, but she would know when she found it.

With growing urgency—had that been footsteps she heard in the corridor?—she pulled the sheets and blanket from the bed and shook them. Then, with a mighty jerk, she dislodged the lumpy-looking mattress and turned it over.

Nothing, nothing. She surveyed the room with a frown, then horror. In the space of five minutes she had caused the chamber to look as though a high wind had blown through.

Quickly Dru replaced the mattress and re-made the bed, but it bore only a semblance of its former neatness. Something was wrong with it, but never in her life had she made a bed, and she was hard put to understand the lack of symmetry. Well, she must correct it, or Duncan would know instantly that his room had been searched.

With a strong feeling of disappointment she pulled at the blanket, but it had become caught on one of the bedcoils. She tugged mightily—*why* had she been unable to find anything?—until the blanket gave way with a sullen rip that sent her spinning toward the wardrobe.

"Of all the nonsensical bothers!" she exploded, and rubbed the back of her head where she had collided with the hard wood of the wardrobe. When the sting had died somewhat, she angrily spread the blanket atop the bed once more, and when the results were even more rumpled than formerly, she slapped the edge of the bed and sat down.

Disconsolately she rested her head in her hands. Several servants passed by in the hall outside, but just now she didn't care if Duncan himself walked through the door. It was too discouraging. All of this searching and nothing to show for it. Could she have been wrong? Or mayhap he was too clever to leave evidence.

She sighed and walked toward the door. Just one final look. . . . No, nothing, only that sheath of wood hanging beneath the wardrobe that had doubtless been dislodged when she struck it.

Narrowing her eyes, telling herself not to hope overmuch, she crossed the room and lay prone before the wardrobe. Only a handspan's distance lay between its bottom and the floor, and she had to turn her head sideways to see underneath. The wood sliver looked to have been cut deliberately, for its edges were too precise to have been formed by accident. Cautiously, hoping not to detach the wood entirely, she reached her hand along the inside. And there, pushed into the crevice formed by the detached wood, she found a piece of paper.

Her heart immediately began to pound. With trembling fingers she removed the note, pulled herself to a seated position, and began to read.

An instant later she sprang to her feet. Tears of disappointment and terror began to spill unheeded from her eyes. She felt her heart fall towards the earth far below.

It was worse, far worse, than she had ever imagined.

How could she—how could they all—have been so deceived? Duncan was evil, so very evil! A villain beyond conception.

But there was no time to stand here thinking of betrayal and hurt. Not while Rissa's life was in danger.

Rissa!

With a little cry, Dru ran from the room.

7

Martha Freecastle and one of the parlourmaids were passing by as Dru burst from Duncan's room. They watched in amazement while she ran past them without explanation.

"Don't ask me," Martha said to the maid. "I've never been able to understand her."

On her flight down the stairs, Dru met Jessup and nearly caused him to fall over the bannister. "Jessup!" she said breathlessly. "Duncan—I fear Duncan means to kidnap Rissa! I don't know when—I mean, she may not be in danger at this moment, but—we must stop him!"

"Now, Lady Druscilla—" Jessup began in disbelief.

"Do not dare to question me, Jessup!" she seethed. "We have not the time. I've found a note in his room which threatens Rissa's safety. And mine," she added in wonder, suddenly realizing the full import of the message.

All of the past days' puzzlements and nagging worries about Duncan fell into a great noxious heap, and Jessup was convinced. "Awright, milady," he said. "Shall I gather the men?"

"Immediately," Dru answered, squeezing her eyes shut in relief.

"Just let me get this wig orf, and we'll be down."

Dru nodded, then continued on her way. She could not wait; the men would be right behind her, but time was of the essence. One moment could make all the difference. It had a year ago. She could not allow a repeat of this past year's guilt. If only Papa had not chosen this day to visit Corfe Castle! But in his bedchamber was a set of pistols ...

Jessup ran to the room he used when duty kept him from his cottage. He ripped the wig from his head and tore at the fastenings of his livery. Probably Lord Cathburn wouldn't mind him ruining the uniform in the service of his daughters, but to be on the safe side ...

Moments later, he fastened the last button of his everyday shirt and reached for the doorknob. At that instant the door sprang inward and Jacobs dashed into the room.

"Your missus, Karl!" Jacobs shouted. "The message boy just came to the Hall to tell you. She's having the baby right now and is calling for you!"

An enormous grin pasted itself onto Jessup's face, and every other thought flew out of his head. "Well, I'll be a cat's hind leg!" he said. "Comin' at last, is he? And about time, too!" He bustled from the room.

A moment later he returned. Jacobs was making his way down the hall, and Jessup grabbed his arm urgently. "Lady Dru asked me to get the men t'gether to go after Duncan, who's with Lady Rissa just now. Says he means t'harm 'er. Do ye gather them, Jim."

"Garn!" Jacobs said in shock, then reflected that he had never liked the new footman. Chest inflating with importance, he added, "I will take care of matters, Karl. Now you go on to Mrs. Jessup."

Jessup nodded in relief and hurried away. Jacobs turned back toward his room, walked a few paces, then turned around again. Exactly how did one gather the men? Should he stand in the hall and shout? And weren't most of the servants already back at duty? What would be the best way to go about it?

He stood indecisively for several long moments, then nodded firmly. All he had to do was tell Mr. Hayes, and he would handle matters. But he must hurry! Too much time had been wasted already.

The footman leaped forward. The carpet runner leapt with him, and, as all inanimate objects seemed to do around him, threw him to the floor. But he was ready for it this time, deciding even in the process of falling that he would use his forward momentum to roll head over heels to his feet, thereby saving the time of rising from bruised knees. If only the carpet had been willing to cooperate with him. But it decided to slip a bit further, and his head hit the floor with all the force a ten-stone man can give.

Jacobs bounced once more and lay sprawled in the servants' hall as one dead.

Dru ran to the stables and shouted for Crickley to saddle Cinnamon, her bay. She started to tell him to gather the groomsmen to aid their search; but one of the new men watched her curiously, and she held her tongue. *Let Jessup handle it when he gets there with the house servants,* she thought. *They can overpower these other villains then.*

Struggling to appear calm, Dru quietly asked Crickley where Lord Sebastian had taken Rissa.

"Don't know fer sure," he said, and removed a large handkerchief to wipe his brow. Dru watched him in an agony of impatience, her feet moving restlessly in the stirrups. "The lord said summat about ridin' over 't the Old Hall."

Dru nodded and clicked Cinnamon into motion. Her

destination was an easy half-hour's ride away. She intended to be there in half that time.

The original Hall had been built over three centuries before. It was little more than a pile of rubble now, but it stood high above the channel and was a special favourite of her sister's. Though Rissa could not enjoy its breathtaking prospect, the winds were constant, and the smells of sea and forest vivid.

Cinnamon was breathing heavily by the time Dru sighted the thick wood that surrounded the ruins on three sides. And there, tied to a tree, were two horses. She was happy to see them, for she had no idea where to look next. With a pat on the horse's neck and a promise for later treats, she slipped from the saddle and tied him next to Satin. Then, with her hand wrapped securely around the cold and deadly article within her pocket, she entered the forest.

Once these trees had formed a park suitable for walking or riding. Now they were densely overgrown, the pines and oaks and ash trees so thick they formed a ceiling betwixt sky and forest floor. It was a dank and dark place, heavy with forgotten secrets and mysteries. But enough visitors came to cause a footpath to fall among the underbrush, and it was this which Dru followed now.

Once she had read a book about the American Indian. They were capable, the book said, of walking soundlessly in the thickest wood. She now attempted to put one foot in front of the other without disturbing the branches and growing things which littered the ground, just as an American Indian would do. It was not possible to achieve complete success, but she was considerably more quiet than she had ever been.

After several moments she heard soft voices, and her steps slowed. A clearing was ahead, where ages ago had been an artificial pond bordered with brick seats. The water had long since dissipated, but many of the bricks remained. Lord Sebastian and Rissa sat there now, talking. Of Duncan there was no sign.

Dru decided the best course would be to stay hidden until the villain's whereabouts could be ascertained. Surely the men would soon arrive, and they would have the strength of many. But she must not make Duncan suspicious and perhaps spur him to precipitate action by making her presence known. She glanced around, assured herself he was nowhere about, and settled behind a tree to wait.

In a moment, however, every thought of Duncan was swept away.

"But I am blind," Rissa was saying, her voice holding more pain than Dru had ever heard her express. "How can you love me, when I am so ... blemished?"

Sebastian caught her to him in a tender embrace. "I care not about that, Rissa. You are all that matters to me."

Rissa's chin trembled, and she leaned her head against his shoulder. "Perhaps I shall regain my sight one day; if that happens, as it did for the lady Charity mentioned ... then, I could be worthy of your love."

"What nonsense you talk!" Sebastian scolded. "I wish you could see again for your sake. But for my part, you are already perfection itself. I cannot banish you from my mind, you know. Do not deny your love for me, if such is what you feel; for in so doing, you condemn me to a greater darkness."

Rissa's eyes glowed with the light of a thousand suns. "I cannot deny that I love you, Sebastian."

The viscount crushed her to him, then cradled her face in his hands and kissed her. Rissa lifted questing fingers toward his face, touching brow, eyes, nose and mouth. "You are very handsome," she said in a wondering voice.

"It does not matter to me, but your countenance is as pleasing as your heart."

Within the puzzle of trees, Dru watched, dumbfounded.

A moment later, Rissa's hands fell reluctantly to her lap. Sebastian watched her, his expression clouding. "Something is wrong."

"What of Dru, Sebastian?" Rissa's hands moved restlessly. "She thinks you mean to offer for her. I cannot hurt her."

He rubbed her shoulder comfortingly. "I am very fond of your sister, and I believe she likes me. But I've thought upon it for awhile now, and I can't imagine her affections are seriously pinned on me." Sebastian placed a finger beneath Rissa's chin and drew her toward him. "In any case, it would not be fair to any of us to let our relationship continue in its old way. Not after this afternoon. I mean to speak to your father straightaway, my dear love."

Rissa leaned away. "I cannot hurt her," she repeated, her mouth in a firm line.

"Rissa . . ." he moaned helplessly.

Dru had heard enough. She walked away from them and toward the ruins, keeping well within the cover of trees; but now she walked without care, an Indian no longer. Stubborn tears stood in her eyes.

"Did you hear something?" she heard Rissa ask.

Sebastian answered, "Some small animal disturbs the leaves, that is all."

Dru continued on, moving faster as she left their range of hearing. The tears began to fall in earnest now, and she wiped at them angrily with the back of her hand. Heedlessly she pushed at broken branches and low-hanging vines; what did a few scratches matter when her heart was breaking?

It had been a long time since she'd had cause to envy

her sister. Dru thought those days would never come again. But it seemed that Rissa had not lost her knack for stealing the gentlemen, even with her disability. And here was the old stabbing pain of old, just as sharp and familiar as if it had always been simmering beneath her skin, merely waiting for an opportunity to burst through.

At least Rissa is unhappy, a voice of reason whispered. She had seemed prepared to refuse Sebastian on Dru's account.

But the viscount has probably convinced her otherwise by now, Dru sneered back. *By leaving, I've doubtless missed a tender scene of reconciliation.*

She shuddered.

Dru had been prepared to sacrifice herself on the altar of marriage for her father's sake. She was going to provide a home for Rissa! Now it looked as if it would be the other way around.

The thought of sharing a home with the two of them made the blood freeze in her veins.

Why, oh why, had her sister divulged her expectations regarding Sebastian? Did he really have to know she had anticipated his making an offer? It seemed a worse betrayal than all the rest.

The roar of the sea was growing louder. Dru had reached the end of the wood, and before her stood the decaying walls of the Old Hall. Only the outer walls remained to continue their losing battle against the elements. Here, on the wind-swept clifftop, no trees dared approach the shrine of broken stone and forgotten dreams.

And there, on the farthest wall and facing outward toward the sea, sat Duncan.

Dru cleared her eyes of tears and placed her hand in her pocket. She would think of Rissa and Sebastian later, for more urgent matters were at hand. She walked forward stealthily, though in truth he would need the ears of a wizard to hear her over the sound of waves crashing below.

When Dru adjudged herself within a safe shooting distance, she cleared her throat and called bravely, "Turn around slowly, you black-hearted imposter."

Duncan swung about immediately. "Lady Druscilla," he said gladly as he moved, but then he saw her face, and his gaze dropped to the pistol she held shakily in front of her.

"Lady Druscilla?" he repeated softly, as though he were unsure it was really she.

"There's no need to look so shocked, Duncan," she said bitterly. "Your terrible plot has failed. I know all."

"You know . . . all?"

"Do not toy with me!" Dru shouted. "I found this note in your room!" She fumbled in her other pocket and held out the crumpled piece of paper. The missive fluttered so violently in the wind that she replaced it at once.

To her great fury, an admiring grin appeared. "You searched my room?"

"Yes, I did, and do not dare to look at me so! How you could—how you could be so depraved, I cannot imagine!" Dru blinked and wiped her eyes with the back of her right hand; seeing the pistol in it, she hurriedly extended the arm again.

"When did you plan to send the note, I wonder?" she continued scornfully. "Was this only one of several drafts? Did they not teach you better penmanship at *Harrow?*"

Anger propelled her forward. "Tell me, Duncan. How did it feel to know you'd blinded a beautiful young lady who had a promising life before her? Was it worth the fifty thousand? Did you plan to do the same to me, or perhaps injure Rissa further, when you threatened to kidnap her again if the tiara is not given to you?"

Her hand was shaking so badly she raised her other arm to support it. "And how could you bear to listen to me accept the blame for Rissa's blindness that day? How you must have—laughed, knowing it was you all along. And after that, you dared to—to—kiss me. How utterly low, Duncan, though why that should surprise me in the light of all I know about you now, I don't know."

Duncan's eyes were amber marbles in the sunshine. Even in the midst of her terrible anger and disillusionment, Dru felt a moment's pain at the hurt she saw there.

"Lady Druscilla, I—"

"Stop, Duncan. I do not wish to hear anything you have to say. Now raise your hands, and walk before me. Remember that I have my father's pistol."

"I did not write that note," he said quietly.

Dru narrowed her eyes. "Of course you did not. The wind merely blew it in your window, and it lodged itself beneath your wardrobe within a sliver of wood." She nodded toward the trees. "You may want to use the walk back to think of more likely excuses. The courts will be most entertained, I am certain."

Seeing he did not move, she jerked the pistol in the direction of the wood and glared at him. Slowly he began to walk forward. "Keep your distance," she warned.

When he drew parallel to her, Dru looked at his fine face and bearing and felt a renewal of the feelings she had known when he kissed her. Such traitorous emotions pushed her to greater fury.

"I hope you hang," she said wrathfully.

"Do you?" he murmured, and then stumbled against a pebble. Before she could react, he snatched the gun from her hand.

Dru cried out in rage and fear. How could she have been so mutton-headed as to relax her guard? She should have known he would have tricked her if given the opportunity. Now she had thrown herself and Rissa, and even the viscount, into his hands.

Duncan held the gun by his side. He looked down at her ashen face and hardened his heart. "Now is my opportunity, is it not, Lady Druscilla?" he asked in measured tones. "I have the gun; there is no one around but two young ladies and an unarmed gentleman who would not fight did I point this pistol at either of his fair companions. Moreover, if I do not act now, the earl's younger daughter will divulge my dark intents, and I shall be exposed. I may have wished for a more opportune time, but now is the time I must move. Do you understand that I cannot delay further?"

Keeping her eyes lowered, she nodded dismally.

"I did not write the note," he repeated, and placed the gun in her hand.

Dru looked at the pistol. She stepped away from his reach and raised it again. He stared at her, his eyes vulnerable and struggling to show no emotion. The gun wavered. She lowered it and slowly replaced it within her pocket. With a hand covering her face, she stumbled toward the stones.

Duncan walked to her side and sat down. Without saying a word, he took her hand within his own.

"What is happening, Duncan?" she sobbed. "What does it all mean?"

He removed his handkerchief and wiped her tears. "You must start remembering your handkerchief, Lady Druscilla, if you're to continue watering your face in this fashion." No sooner had he completed his work than a fresh crop of tears sprang forth. "Noo, noo, lassie. Dinnae hurt yourself so. Hush, noo."

He freed his hand and slipped an arm about her shoulders, pulling her close. She wept awhile longer as he continued to murmur comforting words. Finally she drew several large, shaking breaths and leaned back to stare at him curiously.

"Why do you sometimes sound so very Scottish, Duncan?" It was perhaps not her most urgent question, but surely he would answer this, at least.

"Ah, now you've caught me." He gave her a mischievous look. " 'Tis only when charming damsels in distress catch at my heart. I've even been known to launch into the Gaelic when placed under too much pressure."

"Have you?" Something familiar and nasty stirred within her. "With whom?"

"Only my weeping sister," he pledged, and placed a hand over his heart.

"You have a sister, too. I don't know much about you, Duncan, and I want to know, but at this moment I shall scream do you not explain that note's presence in your room."

"Please do not scream. I'll tell you, but I must obtain permission to do so. Can you not wait, lass, until your father gets home this evening? After dinner, perhaps?"

"You work for my father?"

"Of course." When her eyes became speculative, he added, "All the footmen work for your father."

Dru shot him a look of distaste. "Then nothing remains but for me to go home. And, I suppose, before that . . . speak with Rissa and Sebastian."

His eyes were knowing as he said, "You saw them, did you?"

"I saw them. But they didn't see me."

"Lord Montgomery took me aside and begged I should leave them alone for a few moments. Had it been anyone else but him, I would not have. But he is a trustworthy fellow."

"I suppose he is," she said in a small voice.

He stared at her. "When you saw them, was he . . . ?"

"Lord Sebastian was asking for Rissa's hand."

"And do you find that ... hurtful?"

"You forget yourself," she said, but her voice lacked the spirit of the words. She studied him through her lashes and reconsidered. "Naturally, it hurts me."

"I have watched the three of you together for some time now, and I feared this was coming."

"Would that you had told me. Then I shouldn't feel such a fool."

"Is that what hurts, Lady Druscilla? Wounded pride? Or ..." He swallowed carefully. "Do you love him?"

Of course I love him, she almost said, but then thought: *Not once in the past moments have I mourned the loss of Sebastian himself. I have regretted his knowing that I expected an offer from him; it was galling to think that Rissa had charmed another gentleman away; but Sebastian himself.... He is everything desirable in a suitor, but had he kissed me as he did Rissa, my heart would not have jumped into my eyes as hers did.*

With wonder in her voice she answered, "No, Duncan, I don't love him."

Relief swept through him like a strong wind. "I'm glad."

"Oh?" Dru suddenly became aware of his arm about her shoulders. How comforting he had been, how like a rock. Her spirits had gradually lightened within the shelter of that arm. And though her mind still circled busily about the danger presented by the note, the knowledge that the writer could not be Duncan had cast the anchor off her heart.

The expression in his eyes grew warm. "Yes, I'm glad your affection has not been claimed by the viscount. Because I mean to claim it for myself."

"You do?"

"Yes, you brave, beautiful, *darling* lady." His other arm slipped to her shoulder, and he pulled her close. "You don't think I go about kissing every earl's daughter, do you? For therein would lie the path of madness. But mayhap I *am* mad; if so, I've been driven there by a pair of fiery cat's eyes."

Her lips parted in fascination, and she leaned toward him as though called by a dream. His mouth met hers tenderly at first, then harder as passion grew. For one long moment she was sure her feet left the earth's surface, that she hung suspended above the spinning ball like a cloud. At the same time she knew a growing weakness, and as his lips drifted lower to explore the little hollow of her throat, she leaned backward in joyful compliance.

"This is madness for sure, sweet lass," he murmured between kisses. "But I love you, and love knows no reason."

Dru buried her hands in the thickness of his hair, feeling thankful he did not wear the wig and livery on his rides. She kissed his forehead, his cheek, his lips and thought: *I am out of control! What is happening to me? He will be shocked at my forwardness. But I don't care.*

Duncan was not shocked. "You do love me," he whispered triumphantly, returning kiss for kiss. "Say you love me, sweet lady. Say you will marry me."

Slowly she lowered her hands.

Duncan closed his eyes and pressed his lips to her forehead, then pulled away.

On the horizon, a lone seagull flapped its way toward France. He watched it a long while. Finally he said, "Forgive me. I have assumed too much, thinking you might love me."

"No, Duncan, you have not. It is only that . . ." Dru paused. How could she tell him she'd had a sudden vision of announcing their engagement? "I'd like to introduce my betrothed, Duncan," she would say. "We met while he served as footman at the Hall." And worse: "Rissa and I plan a double ceremony. Yes, you are correct, Rissa's intended is a viscount, but what has that to do with anything?"

"It is only that you cannot love a footman." His smile was cold. "Why should I be surprised? You have already warned me."

She was unwilling to hurt him so. "Duncan, please. A few moments ago I thought you were my worst enemy. I am . . . confused."

"And your confusion has nothing to do with my being a footman, is that it?"

"Why should that matter? Isn't that what you have taught me? But *are* you a footman, Duncan?"

"Why should that matter?" he countered bitterly.

He was impossible. She stood, held a hand toward him beseechingly, then walked a few paces. "I am going home now. Perhaps we can speak of this later."

"Enough has been said already," Duncan replied with quiet determination. He looked at her intently for a moment, then turned his eyes away. She looked so forlorn standing there, with her golden curls tossed into charming disarray by the ocean's breathings. He would remember her like this, and someday the thought would not pain him. But never would he allow himself to be in such a position again. He would never declare himself unless he were sure the young lady reciprocated his feelings. If, indeed, he could ever feel so strongly again. It was not impossible that this green-eyed minx had ruined him for all time.

Dru started to walk toward the trees. On impulse, she curtseyed to him as she would a nobleman. Duncan bowed gravely, then turned back toward the sea.

Just before she entered the wood, he called to her as though suddenly remembering something. "Do you go to join Lady Rissa?"

"No, I think not. I'd really like to be alone. I don't want them to know I saw them."

"You should not be riding unescorted."

"That's all right; before I left I sent Jessup to gather the men. Doubtless I will meet them on the way." Her eyes widened. "The men! Duncan, I have told them you plan to harm Rissa and me! They should be here by now to capture you!"

"Please say you jest."

"No," she moaned. "I do not. I'm sorry, Duncan!"

With a deep sigh he walked toward her. "Let us go, then. It will be best if we are together should they come; otherwise, I may be hanged before the day is done, as you so elegantly wished."

She winced.

The walk back seemed shorter now with Duncan guiding her, though that may have been because his strides were so inconsiderately long.

In honour of her wishes, he approached Rissa and Sebastian alone while she hid among the trees. He was suddenly feeling unwell, he told them, and would they mind if he rode home now?

The viscount said he would be delighted to escort Lady Rissa, and that they would be along in a moment or two. But his expression was strained, Dru noted, as was her sister's; evidently the reconciliation had not taken place.

But things would soon be right between them, if she was the only obstacle. In the light of her own recent activities, she felt guilty at her former reaction. Now she could be happy for Rissa. Now that she knew love herself.

And I do love Duncan, she realized with the impact of a firm truth. *It must be love. That's why I've wondered about him and everything he does. Had anyone else done the things he has, I'd never have noticed. He has not been out of my thoughts since the first day I saw him. Even discounting his imposing presence, even if he were not so handsome and capable of stirring my senses until I scarce know my own name, he is possessed of a character which inspires love. His kindness, his tender regard toward Rissa and myself, and his heart so ready for laughter—all of these recommended him as one worthy of the deepest feeling.*

She smiled at the back of his head as they continued to walk. *No one could make me feel as he does when he kisses me,* she thought. *I would be a fool to let him go, just because he is a footman.*

Wait until I tell him.

But she knew the time wasn't right, for now they must hurry.

When they reached the horses, Duncan lifted her upon Cinnamon, then mounted Satin. "If you don't want Lady Rissa to know you've been here, we'd best meet your mob at a distance," he said, and urged Satin to a gallop. Dru followed closely.

Some twenty minutes later they reached the Hall. Pulling on Cinnamon's reins, Dru looked about her in perplexity. All the horses were in their stalls, and the groomsmen and stableboys went about their work as usual.

"I don't understand," she said in answer to Duncan's questioning look. "Oh, Crickley," she called as the driver entered the yard, "has Jessup been to the stables?"

Crickley removed the straw from his mouth and grinned. "Jessup's been busy, my lady. Mrs. Jessup 'as just given 'im two more little 'uns, all at oncet. Girls, the both of 'em!"

He laughed heartily and went to hold Cinnamon's head while she dismounted. "That's welcome news," she said. "But did he not leave a message with anyone?"

"Not as I know of, Lady Druscilla. Were he suppose
ter?"

"Well . . . it does not matter now."

She looked at Duncan, who dismounted and shrugged
his shoulders. Behind him, in the distance, she thought
she spied the viscount and Rissa. "I must go inside,"
she whispered, and hurried away.

Duncan followed slowly. He would go upstairs to
wash and change before dinner. If his suspicions were
correct, his presence tonight was more crucial than ever.

At that moment Jim Jacobs stumbled from his bed to
stare out the attic window. Something was troubling
him; there was something he had meant to do before the
carpet attacked him. Though it was nice to have the afternoon off to nurse his wounded head.

He saw Lady Dru rush into the Hall, then watched
Duncan following her. *Duncan!* Jessup had told him to
call the men together!

His knees trembled. The others were always laughing
at him for his clumsiness. But to have neglected so important a mission was no laughing matter. What would
they do to him now?

It was too late to call the men together to search for
Duncan, because there he was. Perhaps even now he
came upstairs. Here was a chance to redeem his failure,
was it not?

Think, Jim, think! he told himself.

Duncan climbed the last stair and turned down the
hall, weary in heart and mind. His door stood ajar,
thanks no doubt to Lady Druscilla's explorations. Seeing his childishly made bed, he chuckled in spite of
himself and closed the door behind him.

And never saw the chair which descended upon his
head with the energy of a man possessed behind it.

"I've done it!" Jacobs shouted. He looked at the body
lying beside the bed and repeated in a softer voice,

"I've—done it." His hand flew to his throat. "You're not—you're not dead, are you, Duncan?" he said in sudden remorse, and knelt beside him, pressed his ear to his chest, then sighed in relief. "You'll be all right."

When his victim groaned and began to move, Jacobs jumped to his feet and looked around wildly.

He shook his head at the chair. No more violence for him, never again. First and only time, please God; it had not been as satisfying as he thought.

Then he looked at the bed and grinned. "I've got to tie you up so I can get some help, Duncan," he explained. Swiftly he pulled off the bedding and began to work.

Some moments later, Jacobs stepped back to admire his handiwork. Duncan's arms and legs were tied together behind his back tighter than a trussed chicken. It was a good job, he decided, even if the man had regained himself enough to speak. He couldn't like what he was saying, though, so he marched to the wardrobe, removed a shirt, and gagged Duncan's mouth.

"I'll be back in a minute, old fellow," Jacobs said. "Now don't go looking at me like that. What did you expect, wanting to hurt the ladies and all? Stop that wriggling about." When the motion continued he added, "All right, I'll stop it for you, then." He tore another strip off the sheet and tied Duncan's feet to one of the wardrobe's legs.

"You'd best stop moving about like a snake or you'll have the furniture on your head," Jacobs warned, then moved toward the door.

But it was too late. Already the wardrobe was teetering toward the prone man lying helplessly below. Such a heavy piece might crush all his ribs, or even kill him, Jacobs thought. And it would be his fault!

With a swiftness borne of guilt, Jacobs plunged across the room to catch the wardrobe. But the chair caught his foot instead, and he fell across Duncan's body.

He had time only to register the look of horror in his captive's eyes before the wardrobe fell on them both, and darkness took Jacobs once more.

8

That evening, Pizzy thought Lady Dru was up to old ways, so demanding was she, excepting she was so cheerful about it. First it was on and off with her dress, for here was a wrinkle, and there a spot. Then it was the slippers: first the ivory, then the green. And her hair! Lady Dru insisted it be washed, pomaded, and wrapped to bring out the shine. When had she ever gone to so much trouble for a simple dinner? Even if two gentlemen did plan to attend.

But it was impossible not to be pleased with the results. Lady Dru wore her prettiest new gown, never before worn. Made of emerald brocade, it was trimmed in rows of cascading Brussels lace at the hem and puffed sleeves. The decolletage showed a pretty expanse of bosom that was further enhanced by a jade pendant set in gold. Tiny jade stones graced her earlobes, and a green velvet bandeau highlighted her hair. Around her shoulders she wore a gauze shawl decorated in a floral pattern.

Viewing herself in the full-length mirror, Dru chewed her lip doubtfully. "Am I fit, Pizzy?"

"Dear, you've never been lovelier," the maid replied tiredly. "Don't know when I've see a finer looking lady."

"Rissa is, without even trying," Dru said loyally, even though her vanity still smarted from the afternoon's revelations.

Pizzy knew better than to dispute her, though privately she thought the ladies of equal beauty. But then, it was hard to be objective when her evaluation was coloured by a carefully hidden sense of competition with Martha Freecastle.

Dru thanked her for her service and walked to her sister's room, only to find that Martha had already escorted Rissa to the library. Descending the stairs, Dru forgot her concern over her appearance and became nearly overwhelmed by anticipation. Tonight Duncan would explain his mysterious actions; and all ladylike reticence aside, she would tell him she returned his love. Furthermore, she would give her blessing to Rissa and Sebastian and bring them happiness. Her father would be besieged by suitors, which would in turn make possible his own marriage. They would all rejoice together. It could not be better.

Except for that terrible note, of course. But surely it would prove to be no more than a misunderstanding or a cruel joke. Nothing could mar the happiness of such a night.

She turned toward the library and paused. Instead of finding Duncan as she had expected, Alfred and Matthews attended the doorway, their expressions rife with martyrdom. Puzzled, she approached the butler, who was standing by the front door.

"Hayes, where is Duncan?" she asked.

The servant looked toward the ceiling. "I know not, Lady Druscilla," he said in tones bespeaking much long-suffering. "We experience a lack of footmen this evening. Mr. Jessup is, uh, celebrating the arrival of twin girls, and Jacobs and Duncan have gone missing." He sniffed regretfully. "One never knows with servants.

I've had to call in the two you see there, and it is not their night for duty."

"But they are usually so faithful," Dru said, disturbed. "I suppose someone has been sent to their rooms to look for them?"

"Yes, my lady. Neither answered. But tomorrow they will account for it, I assure you."

She murmured a placating response and turned toward the library. Where could Duncan be? Surely he had not met with an accident, for he had been directly behind her when she entered the house.

Suddenly a wonderful thought occurred. What if he planned to attend dinner dressed in gentleman's clothing, as a real guest? What if her discovery of the note had caused him to realize he could continue his masquerade no longer? Perhaps tonight he would reveal himself to be a duke or a marquis who had taken a footman's disguise in order to find a worthy bride unimpressed by riches and titles, not unlike the enchanted prince who was delivered from his frogly spell by a kiss.

But why would he then bury himself in a house where lived only two young ladies not given to many entertainments that would bring other females to his presence? a little niggling voice argued. *For in so doing he certainly would have limited his range of choice. And what of the note?* But she dismissed the thoughts and entered the library with a determined look of cheer.

It was fortunate she did so, for her entrance brightened the atmosphere of forced conviviality within the room. Rissa's side had been claimed by James Burke, she noted, while Lord Sebastian watched them moodily from across the room, his attention barely caught by the earl's account of his day at Corfe Castle.

While she made her curtsey, Dru felt heavy-hearted seeing the brave expression on Rissa's face. Though she attended James's conversation with polite interest, she could not hide her tense sadness from Dru.

I should have found time to speak with her earlier, Dru thought guiltily, *instead of spending so much time dressing for Duncan, who is not even here to see me.*

Pulling her gaze from Rissa's countenance, she asked her father, "Does Mrs. Tweetle not join us?"

"Bless her, she was worn out with our travels today and cried off, but she sends her regrets to all," he replied.

Dru's thoughts were so preoccupied that she felt not even a twinge of relief at the announced absence. Her immediate goal was to relieve Rissa and Sebastian from their unhappiness, but how to accomplish it in such a setting? The presence of James complicated matters, though in truth she could not imagine how to go about it were he not there.

A major deterrent was her wish to avoid disclosing her knowledge of Sebastian's proposal to Rissa; one had to salvage a little pride, after all. But she could hardly say to him, "Lord Sebastian, on the off chance that you should ever propose to me, I have decided that we do not suit." Nor could she announce, "I've decided to marry the footman," because he was not present to support her in the inevitable earthquake that would follow *that* news.

Perhaps she should flirt outrageously with James and give Sebastian a disgust of her. But Rissa would suspect something was amiss at such uncharacteristic behaviour.

Dru grew so thoughtful that she was in danger of becoming as morose as the two thwarted lovers. Even the earl was affected, so much so that when Hayes entered the room to announce dinner, he greeted him with exuberant relief.

Sebastian immediately turned from her father and herself with the obvious intent to assist Rissa to the dining room. But seeing that James already escorted her, the viscount checked his steps and offered his arm to Dru instead. He displayed a remarkable control, Dru thought. Only the redness of his cheeks betrayed his strong feeling.

She was relieved to see the small dining parlour was in use. The room's large round table permitted of general conversation. A plan was forming in her mind, and hopefully such would prove useful.

When they were seated, Dru said, "Last evening's entertainment was exceptional in quality, do you not agree? How unusual, but pleasing, it is to see a married couple so equally matched in talent and charm."

The others murmured agreeably. While Hayes supervised the footmen in the serving of the first course, Dru continued, "Moreover, their love for one another is obvious. Yet I have heard it said that love is the poorest reason for marriage; one must consider social standing and financial advantage first." She dipped her spoon into her soup, then looked up with sparkling eyes. "I wonder . . . what think you?"

She looked at her companions expectantly. Rissa wore a puzzled frown, James watched her with bright eyes, and Sebastian stared at the tablecloth. Finally the earl cleared his throat and said, "As the only one here who's been wed, I can tell you that love ain't enough. If you're meaning love like most young ladies do, that swoony kind of mush-eyed stuff, it won't last. No more than six weeks on the outside, I'd say. Got to have something else besides."

Astonished, Dru said, "Papa! Do you mean to say you never loved Mama?"

"Did you hear me say that? Naturally I loved her. But our marriage was agreed upon after we'd met only a few times. Hardly knew the gel when we was wed. But your grandparents made the arrangements with an eye to dowries and bloodlines, so we suited in those ways. The rest came later, after we'd had time together. Became great friends."

Dru could not like the turn the conversation was taking. She was great friends with Sebastian, and that did not at all serve the argument she hoped to bring forth. Yet she was intrigued by these revelations of her father.

"Is that how you feel about Mrs. Tweetle?" she couldn't help asking. "You are . . . great friends?"

"Well now, Druscilla!" he said, flustered. "Don't go rushing the horse over the hedge." Then, without meaning to, he thought of Mrs. Tweetle's soft brown eyes, her round, neat figure and pleasing ways. He recalled how his heart thumped in anticipation every time he stood outside her door. Maybe he was getting soft in his old age, but he couldn't recollect ever feeling that way about the girls' mother. However, such a thing could never be admitted, so he coughed to cover his confusion and ended by saying, "But of course, Mrs. Tweetle and I are friends."

James said, "I agree with you, Lord Cathburn, that married partners should be friends. But," he added, his wide, expressive eyes looking apologetic, "I think it often happens that friendship comes later, after love sets it into motion. But real love—and I speak here of the passionate, all-consuming sense of the word, where one would sacrifice all, and dedicate oneself to the other, where one cannot exist without the presence of the beloved—is the best basis of marriage." His face became serious. "Not riches, not the suitability of one partner for the other, but that unknown, unexplained attraction which impels one person toward another. Some loves are destined, and destiny cannot be resisted."

Dru's heart began to race. The intensity of James's words, so calmly yet fervently spoken, made her think yearningly of Duncan. But she set her feelings aside and asked, "What about you, Lord Sebastian? Have you formed an opinion?"

The viscount, who had been watching James carefully as he spoke, slowly removed his gaze to look at Dru. "I bclicve there cannot be a valid obstacle to the joining of two kindred souls. Not if they both truly love one another." He lowered his lashes and turned almost casually in Rissa's direction. "But Lady Rissa has not shared her thoughts."

"I agree with you, Lord Sebastian," Rissa said softly, "with one exception. If that love is hurtful to someone else, nothing good will come of it. For always there would be that knowledge: happiness bought at the expense of another."

"Oh, pshaw, Clarissa!" the earl cried. "No one 'twould ever get married, then. Mind how often a young lady is pursued by two suitors. Is she not to choose one over the other for fear of hurting the rejected one?"

"I did not mean that exactly," she said in fainter tones.

Dru watched her with concern. She must end this now or Rissa would have one of her headaches; indeed, she probably endured one at this very moment. Rissa had that pinched look about the nostrils; she was growing pale, and not one bite of food had passed her lips.

Leaning back to allow Alfred space to replace her soup with a dish of turbot and peas in white sauce, Dru forced enthusiasm into her voice and said, "I don't believe anyone has asked for *my* opinion."

With a fond look, Lord Cathburn said, "Tell us, my dear."

"I think there are many kinds of love, some of which are more suitable for marriage than others." She paused to make sure Sebastian and Rissa listened. When they both looked curiously in her direction, she continued, "It seems to me the kind of love of which James spoke is the best start for marriage. If that love fades into friendship in later years, well, perhaps it would be disappointing but a comfort; at least it would be better than detesting one another. However, if a marriage begins with feelings of friendship, would it not be difficult to generate warmer regard?"

Dru took a deep breath, leaned toward Sebastian and touched his arm, an action which seemed to alarm him. "To make an example: In the weeks I've known Lord Sebastian, I've grown most fond of him, but it is a fondness one has for a brother, nothing more. Though I look forward to spending time in his presence, would that not be a paltry beginning for a wedding? Not that you had intended to ask me, of course!" she added with a giggle worthy of the stage.

The viscount was unable to disguise the hope that illuminated his every feature. Immediately he looked at Rissa, whose lips had parted in wonder and growing joy.

Without removing his gaze from Rissa, Sebastian said in a voice wildly imitative of injured pride, "So you think of me as a brother, do you? That is all?"

Dru patted his arm and removed her hand. "Yes, but such a brother as to make all sisters everywhere sigh in envy!"

"You think of him as a brother?" Rissa echoed, not quite able to believe, her brow furrowing as she recalled their many conversations concerning Dru and her future with the viscount.

"I'll admit I was overwhelmed at first by the charm and elegance of bearing which the viscount possesses in great quantities," Dru said carefully, wishing her sister were more easy to fool. "What young lady would not be? But as time passed, there came not that . . . magic . . . which seems to be within the hands of higher powers and not for humanity to dispense at will." With a mischievous look she concluded, "I trust I do not offend you, Lord Sebastian?"

"Offend? Of course you offend!" the viscount said, but the smile splitting his face gave lie to the words. "Yet I hope my heart shall mend eventually."

Rissa heard the smile in his voice and answered it with a resplendent one of her own.

Lord Cathburn, who had nursed many hopes for Dru and the viscount, rested his forehead in his hand and groaned.

James watched them all with intelligent intensity, his gaze most frequently settling upon Rissa. As her face brightened, as the conversation grew increasingly frivolous and light-hearted, his expression became proportionately grim.

While the dinner slowly passed through four removes and ended with cheese, nuts, and the earl's omnipresent apple tarts, Dru had occasion to wish she were a better person. There had been joy aplenty in watching Sebastian and Rissa as they struggled to contain their ballooning happiness, but as soon as the first novelty had worn thin, her own concerns came to the forefront, and she found herself hardly able to think of them at all.

Where was Duncan?

Gone were her hopes that he would burst into the room in his elegant Bond Street clothes to carry her off in a golden carriage. In their place were worries. Was he all right? And worse: the suspicions, those tiresome accompaniments to her thoughts over the past weeks. They wriggled through her brain like ugly, squiggling worms and proved that she did not yet trust him entirely. And that was the most downturning thought of all.

What if he *had* written the note? Perhaps this afternoon had merely been a quickly thought plan to delay her from telling all. At this very moment he could be calling his men together to storm the house demanding tiara, Rissa, herself, or maybe all three.

Finally even the earl had eaten his fill, and Dru came to attention. In the ordinary way of things, the gentlemen would now enjoy Spanish cigars and port while she and Rissa retired to the library. Then, judging from the eager look on Sebastian's face, he would capture the earl for a session of marriage-making in his study. Well, none of those things were going to happen, at least not until she spoke with her father.

Before the earl could signal her to leave the room, Dru put on her best smile and said, "Papa, I must see you for a moment in your study." Without allowing time for his protest, she rose to her feet. "I beg you will excuse us for a few moments," she said to the others, "but I have just thought of a household matter which must be attended to immediately. Please make use of the library if you wish to be more comfortable."

Lord Cathburn gave his guests a helpless look and followed, though he protested mightily when they reached the hall. When he entered his study and Dru closed the door firmly behind him, however, all thought of protest died. Seldom had even she looked so determined.

"Have you any idea where Duncan can be?" she asked urgently.

"Is this all you're about? We've not the time to be discussing the footman, Druscilla; there's guests to be entertained."

"Do you know where he is?"

"Hound's tooth, child, but you're persistent. No, I don't know where he is." He looked thoughtful. "Fact is, I've been wondering that m'self."

"Did he not see you this afternoon when he returned from the ride with Rissa?"

"No, but then I was late; had barely time to change before dinner."

She bit her lower lip. "Who is he, Papa?"

"Aw, don't start that again. He's just a footman, don't I tell you that every time you ask?"

"Yes, and not once have you met my eyes when you said it. I fear that you have been telling me stories, Papa."

"Well!" he said huffily, and sat in the leather chair behind his desk. "Things have got to a far pass when my own gel talks so to her father. Don't know what I've done to deserve such a lack of respect. Wouldn't have tolerated it in my men for an instant."

A soft hand passed by his shoulder and laid a piece of paper on the desk. "This is why I speak so. I found it hidden in Duncan's room this afternoon and confronted him with it. He promised to explain all at dinner, but told me he would obtain your permission first. One of you is spinning tales, and I must know which, for if it is Duncan, then I believe Rissa and myself to be in the gravest danger."

Lord Cathburn stared at the note, then looked at his daughter. "And what business took you to Duncan's room?"

"The business of trying to discover something about this man!" she cried. "No one will tell me anything, and I grow weary of wondering. Besides, that is of little importance. The pertinent thing is this threatening message!"

The earl rubbed his forehead and sighed. "Very well, child, very well. Always your mind has pleased me, so how can I be surprised that you made this discovery? Yet I heartily wish you had not."

"Why?" she challenged. "Would it not be better to be

forewarned of the danger?" She made a face. "Or did you judge me too weak-hearted to bear the worry?"

"No, Druscilla; not to protect you from worry, but Clarissa. Didn't doubt for a minute that you could tolerate the situation, but you know how delicate your sister's become. Thought it would send her over the edge to think she might be subjected to this criminal again. And I knew you'd not be able to keep it from her; the two of you are closer than spots on an owl. And as to the forewarned part, of what use could that be? You're a fearless mite, but there's little you could do in your own defense. That's what I hired Duncan for."

"You hired Duncan to . . . protect us?" she breathed, her heart beginning to roll in delight. "He is not the kidnapper? He is not a footman?"

"Not a bit of it." He fumbled at the papers within his desk. " 'Tis here somewhere, I know it. Now hold onto your slippers, child, I'll find it. Ah! Here 'tis."

He handed her a card, which she read with shaking hands:

MY LORD'S INQUIRIES
Discreet Investigations
No. 12 Edward Street
London

———

Lord Kyle Duncan

"A lord! He is a lord!" *And not a footman,* her heart sang. Hadn't she always known?

"Yes, a baron's son he is; owns an estate in Essex, near Tilbury. But it's a decrepit affair, so he told me. Been practically abandoned all these years, but he wants to restore it."

"So he works to earn necessary funds," Dru said, her mind spinning. Perhaps his father had gambled his fortune away, and poor Duncan must work for a living. Well, she would soon save him from *that* necessity. Suddenly remembering their conversations, she said, "But, Papa, I thought he was raised in Scotland."

"He was. His mother is the daughter of a Scottish laird. The baron was bewitched by the Highlands when they visited her home, so when her father died, he took management of the castle in Cromarty. Even took his name."

"Duncan owns a castle?" she squealed in delight.

He shrugged. "Yes, now that his sire's dead, though he prefers England. But what's it matter? Point is, Duncan's built a reputation in London for good work. Found Lady Summer's lost diamonds—the maid stole 'em; located a lost child. That sort of thing. Kind of a private police agency."

"But why impersonate a footman, Papa? Is that what you required of him?"

"Once he knew I was bound on secrecy, 'twas his very own idea. The man can't be everywhere at once, nor can his men. But who is more able to watch, and be in a position to protect, than a servant? Most people don't even see 'em. That way, too, he could accompany you both to other houses. Gather more clues without being noticed. Could also investigate the servants. Lots more freedom to get about quietly than if he'd come as a guest."

"But ... why should he need to investigate the servants, or other people's business? I don't understand."

"Now this is the hardest thing, Druscilla, to say. But Duncan believes the kidnapper is known to us."

She looked at him solemnly. "Rissa mentioned as much at our picnic. She remembered something the villain said which made her think he knew her."

He nodded. "Yes, but 'tis not the only reason. This villain, as you well call him, knows us intimately. He knew when to snatch Clarissa in London, and where. And he knows we keep the tiara at the Sussex estate, since that's the birthplace of the Selbys and its traditional home; that's why he sent this note. For what's the logic in sending a note of warning? If he wanted the Selby tiara, why not ask for it immediately? No, he knew we needed time to send for it, a fact only known by a few. But as soon as I got the note, I sent for Duncan as well as the tiara."

"So the Selby is here?"

"In the safe in this very room."

"Now I understand why Duncan watched me at the Winters's house. I suppose he didn't know much about Sebastian at the time," she mused. "And it explains the guard following us on our drive as well. But why on earth did I find him in the cloak room last night?"

The earl snorted. "This morning he told me you caught 'im at it. He was searching to find scraps of paper—anything that might have a sample of handwriting which he could compare with the note. Said it was not likely, and he met with no success. But according to Duncan, much investigating is like that. Persistence is rewarded eventually though, he says."

"I thought he robbed the guests," she said with a little smile.

"So he said. We had a good laugh over it."

Dru felt an instant's pique at being the hapless object of their amusement, but her good spirits rapidly returned.

"I'm glad to know Duncan is not a villain after all," she said, knowing it for an understatement, but unwilling to reveal more of her feelings to her father before speaking with Duncan. Thinking of him now, she felt suddenly shy. How could she face him, knowing all the terrible things she'd said and imagined?

Had it merely been hours ago that she held him at pistol-point and wished him hanged?

If her father noticed her flaming cheeks, he gave no sign. "Remember, Druscilla," he said firmly, "not a word to Rissa. Let us return to our guests now."

Dru put a restraining hand on his arm. "But don't you think it would be wise to warn Lord Sebastian of the danger?"

The earl flinched at the name as though she had plunged a knife through his heart. With some bitterness he replied, "Why, child? Why should he know? 'Tis not as though he'll be around all that much after you dashed his hopes at dinner."

"Dashed his hopes? Oh! You mean—" she gave an embarrassed giggle, then stopped in confusion. It was not possible to explain about Rissa and the viscount without revealing the knowledge gained this afternoon. And while pride might be overcome for such a reason, loyalty could not; these joyous tidings were not hers to bestow.

As she struggled to create a sensible reply, a rapid knocking was heard at the door. Lord Cathburn had scarce opened his mouth to answer it when Hayes burst into the room.

"I beg your pardon, my lord," the butler said, his usual calm demeanour disturbed by strong emotion. "Alfred informs me some half-dozen groomsmen and gardeners have demanded the key to Duncan's room and are threatening to tear down the door do they not receive it." He took a deep breath. "It is a most unusual situation and I thought to ask your advice, since you, and not I, employed these servants." And from the expression in his eyes, Dru could plainly see what he thought of *that* arrangement.

"Give them the key, then," the earl said sensibly.

Hayes bowed, the stiffness of his neck shouting disapproval. "My lord, if I might remind you, one of the advantages promised servants in your employ is the guarantee to privacy. It has been our rule to never unlock doors in the help's quarters, except for the cleaning maids when they go about their duty. Besides, I had the pot boy knock on his door earlier, and there was no answer." He sniffed. "I do not think it will sit well with the lower orders to observe these newer fellows exhibiting such a privilege."

Lord Cathburn did not trouble to hide his exasperation. "Then I shall have to do it myself," he said, and bustled past the startled butler.

"Oh no, my lord, I didn't mean—"

"And I will go with him," Dru said, a determined look on her face. For now she was more worried than ever. If Duncan's men were anxious to such an extent, then there must be cause for alarm.

When they reached the kitchen, she saw the regular staff turn guiltily back to their tasks; but it was obvious the spectacle of Duncan's men had caught their attention, and they cast many a surreptitious glance in their direction. As a chastened Hayes fetched the key from the pantry, a freckled, sturdy-looking young man from the group stepped close to the earl, glanced at Dru and the kitchen workers, and began to speak in a soft voice.

When she moved closer to hear better, the young man ceased talking and looked at her. Lord Cathburn turned aside, seemed surprised to see she stood behind him, and waved the servant on. "Never mind," he said impatiently. "She knows all, as anyone with sense would know she was bound to do. Speak your mind, er—"

"Doug Harris, my lord," he whispered. "Anyway, he didn't report to us two hours ago as he ought, so we began our search around the stables and grounds. We thought to check his room, then mount a larger search if he's not there."

"Very well," the earl said, and accepted the key from Hayes. "Though it would surprise me to find him in his room. Surely Duncan would answer the knock at his door." Shaking his head, he began to puff his way up the stairs.

Dru quickly maneuvered herself behind him, and the men followed. She wished her father would move faster. She almost was tempted to place her arms upon his back and push, for a sense of urgency was growing within her. But at last they stood before Duncan's room, and the earl placed the key in the lock.

Dru gave a little cry of horror when the door swung open. While she stood motionless, the men pushed past her to lift the wardrobe from the two figures beneath it.

"What in Cain's dreams can be behind this?" Lord Cathburn demanded.

Dru kneaded her hands together and watched them remove Jacobs to the bed. His head lolled to the side and he smiled sweetly, though he did not regain consciousness. Her eyes returned frantically to Duncan, who was being released from his bindings by several men at once.

"Why is he tied?" the earl persisted, concern giving his voice an irritable edge. "Is he dead?"

A moan escaped her lips at such a thought, and she brushed past the circle of servants to kneel beside Duncan. His face was very pale against the dark stubble of beard that had grown since she last saw him. Oblivious to those standing around her, Dru leant toward him and called his name, then touched his cheek. And was rewarded at last by a pair of amber eyes slowly opening.

Confusion gave way to tenderness in those eyes as he saw her, only to be replaced by a guarded expression; then, full awareness returned. He moved his head to take in the crowd around him. "Well, give us a hand up, then," he said hoarsely. "I dinnae think I'll do it on me oon."

Tears of gratitude welled up in her eyes, and she moved aside to allow the men room to assist him. After a moment of muffled groans, he stood shakily to his feet, stretching and bending and moving his legs to renew circulation.

"Break anything?" the earl asked. "If not, I'll thank you to ease my curiosity."

"Everything seems in working order," Duncan replied painfully. "But someone needs to tell that poor fool yonder that I'm not meaning to kidnap your daughters." He darted only the quickest of glances at Dru, then turned back to the earl. "He caught me by surprise when I returned to the room. Hit me over the head with that chair."

Dru clapped a hand to her mouth, lowered her head, and watched her protector with a shamed expression. But he did not look at her.

"Well, well," the earl said consideringly. "What a surprise you turned out to be, Jim Jacobs." He touched one of the men on the shoulder. "Go tell Hayes to fetch the physician for our brave footman."

The man left to do his bidding. Duncan watched him, then suddenly exclaimed, "Why are you all here? Who guards Lady Rissa?"

Lord Cathburn said soothingly, " 'Tis all right. Lord Sebastian and James Burke are with her downstairs."

Duncan's pale face became ashen. "Do not say so," he breathed, and ran from the room.

Dru exchanged an alarmed look with her father. Spurred on by the investigator's urgency, they both dashed toward the stairs; but it was a race they shared and quickly lost to Duncan's men.

By the time they reached the hall, Hayes was expostulating in injured tones. The group gathered around him was almost threatening in their tense postures.

"But Mr. Burke has been gone almost a half-hour," he was saying. "He left as soon as Lord Sebastian and Lady Clarissa set out to walk in the garden. And no, they are still out there; though why it is any of your business, I cannot imagine."

Immediately they rushed into the library and out the french doors. Dru and the earl followed, and the bewildered butler trailed behind. They ran heedlessly among the flowers and shrubbery and benches, calling and calling Rissa's name.

In a moment we will find them sitting beneath a tree, Dru prayed silently. *They will be so startled and amused to see us searching for them. Please let it be so.*

But it was not to be.

The frantic search continued for several long moments. Finally a distressed voice called from the far corner of the garden, and Dru's heart constricted at the sound.

"Over here!" Harris was shouting. He stood beside a bench sheltered beneath a great spreading oak. A hedge of hawthorn bordered the bench on one side. At first Dru could see nothing, but as she ran breathlessly on, the still form lying on the ground became visible.

Even in the darkness and long shadows, she could not fail to recognize Sebastian.

Duncan was the next to arrive, and he lifted the groaning viscount to a sitting position. A grievous wound on the back of his head bled freely. Upon the grass lay the weapon, a cudgel carelessly thrown aside. Sebastian blinked several times, but his eyes refused to focus. He slipped toward unconsciousness again, but Duncan was unwilling to surrender his witness, and he gently slapped the young lord's cheeks and called his name.

"Sebastian, where is Rissa? Where has she gone? Could you see who took her?"

The viscount struggled to open his eyes. "Rissa . . ." he breathed. "Rissa is . . . gone?" He leaned forward, then sank back again, his eyes full of agony.

"Och, well, he'll noo be helping us any," Duncan said, his mouth a grim line. "But what's this?" He pulled a piece of paper from Sebastian's jacket, a paper obviously meant to be found, since it lay only halfway within the pocket.

"What does it say?" Dru asked, her voice breaking with emotion.

Duncan read it, then turned hopeless eyes upon the earl. "You are to bring the tiara to Cathburn Harbour at three of the clock this morning, alone. A sailing vessel will be anchored offshore, and a rowboat will be found on the beach. After rowing the tiara to the halfway point, abandon the boat and swim for shore. Someone will gather the tiara and return Rissa to the rowboat." He ran shaking fingers through his hair. "I'm so sorry, Lord Cathburn, Lady Druscilla. So very, very sorry."

The earl extended a hand toward the bench and sat wearily. " 'Tis not your fault, Duncan. I don't blame you."

Tears rained upon Dru's cheeks. "Rissa," she cried. "That this could happen to you again. Life cannot be so cruel. Why was it not me?"

Duncan lifted a hand toward her, then let it fall. He became intent upon the note again. "Look at this, Druscilla," he said. "Do you recognize the stationery?"

"It is our own," she said between sobs.

"Meaning that someone used it hurriedly. Someone with free access to the library."

"A—a servant?" she asked, not wanting to believe the implication.

"James Burke," he returned.

"But—but that's impossible! His feeling toward Rissa was of the most tender. And beside that, he left immediately following her rejection of his proposal last year. He was in America when she was kidnapped!"

"That's what he wished you to believe, but in my investigations of the neighboring houses, I became curious about him and had a man check the passenger rosters in London for that time. Only yesterday did I receive word that the date for his departure was two weeks *after* the kidnapping."

"Dear God, can it be believed?" the earl said, and his voice sounded very old to Dru's ears. "We have known the boy all his life."

"I believe he acted ahead of his plan this evening," Duncan said, his eyes taking on a thoughtful light. "Something precipitated him to action, for otherwise he would not have used the Cathburn stationery. If that is so, he is liable to make another mistake. Perhaps everything is not in place at the harbour as well. If God wills, we shall yet prevail this night."

Dru watched him, wanting to believe. He looked at her briefly and nodded with a determined confidence. But when he turned his eyes away, she felt her heart sink. Was it a decrease in his certainty that caused him to fail to meet her eyes, or was it something more? Though she could think of scarce aught but her sister's terrible plight, still she shivered at the distance she sensed in his regard.

9

Within moments of their moving Sebastian within the house, Duncan and his men were gone. No time could be lost, he had said. Mayhap they could intercept Burke before he took Clarissa on the ship. If not, they must allow time to station themselves secretly at the harbour. The note demanded the earl's solitary attendance, and until the young lady was safe, they must appear to follow his directions.

"Do we not tempt fate by going against him at all?" Lord Cathburn had asked.

"We dare not do otherwise," Duncan replied. "The man is too unpredictable."

The earl had nodded, and the men rode off, the horses' hoofbeats sounding like thunder in Dru's ears.

She said nothing to Duncan before he left. There had not been the opportunity. The men seemed so officious and capable in their speech and rapid, purposeful movements. She had stood aside, her hurting, stunned mind hardly taking in anything she observed. She felt to be of no more use than a child.

Yet she wanted to bid him godspeed, at least; to tell him to take care. But he had not at any time looked in her direction. So she said nothing.

When the last of the guard disappeared into the darkness, she and her father returned inside. The butler and several other servants stood grouped in the hall, their faces registering shock and confusion. The earl began to apprise them of the situation, and Dru entered the library to attend Sebastian.

He lay in a half-reclining position upon the sofa while the housekeeper bathed his wound. At Dru's appearance he was stirred to a semblance of animation, though it was plain he kept his eyes open with only the most valiant force of will.

Dru pulled a footstool beside him and said, "How does he, Mrs. Ames?"

"The bleeding's almost stopped, my lady," the housekeeper replied. "I hope the surgeon will arrive soon."

Sebastian extended a hand toward Dru, and she clasped it within her own. "What has happened?" he whispered. "Rissa . . . is she all right?"

"Rissa will be fine," she declared. "Do not talk, Sebastian; you'll hurt yourself more."

"We were sitting in the garden," he said, his voice full of confusion, "and she heard a small sound in the shrubbery. I heard nothing. But . . . I turned to look, and that is all I remember."

Dru patted his shoulder. "I know. Do not think about it. Rest now."

"Someone . . . struck me. They have not taken Rissa, have they? Dru, tell me. Where is she?"

Dru was spared making an answer by the arrival of the doctor, who requested she leave while he made his examination. When she re-entered the hall, she was surprised to see her father was no longer there. Hayes informed her he had repaired to his study.

She hardly recognized the voice that answered her knock at the study door; and when she entered the room, she was dismayed to see the dejected, aged-looking figure of her father slumped in a chair by the fire. In his lap he held an intricately carved box of mahogany with ivory inlay. His eyes were fixed upon it with a dreadful intensity, and he did not look up at her approach.

"Come and see, Druscilla," he said. "Come view the object that's caused this great calamity. I reckon 'twill be your first and last time."

She rushed to kneel beside his chair, her heart in a flutter for him. It was one thing to suffer her own sadness, but harder still to bear her father's. She placed her hand upon his arm and blinked back tears.

He lifted the lid. Despite the great depression of her spirits, she could not suppress a small gasp. Never had she seen so lovely an article wrought by human hands. The tiara seemed to be crafted entirely of diamonds, so finely made was its framework; the semi-circle of tiny stones sparkled against the red velvet lining like a vision of fairyland. At the highest point, in the center, lay a single diamond so perfect and large that she could only speculate as to its cost. Of its symmetry and beauty, there was no reckoning.

" 'Tis a fine-looking thing, there's no denying," he said. "But when compared to your sister's well-being, I have no love for it."

Dru could only agree. Yet her mind circled with questions. She debated briefly whether or not her father could answer them, or whether or not she should trouble him further; but the questions would not be denied.

"Papa, why would James want the tiara? If the kidnapper is James, that is; and I'm not entirely convinced it is he."

"I've had my doubts as well, but Duncan's persuaded me. Why else would James lie about his departure date?"

"Maybe he feared he would be connected to the kidnapping for some reason. Perhaps it was only a precaution."

"He'd have done better to appear in Town, then, during the time of her capture. 'Twas no secret to our acquaintances. She was gone a week, you know. No, child, if such were his fears, he was a fool to disappear. Much as it pains me, I believe Duncan has the right of it."

"But if it is he, why the Selby tiara? If he seeks funds, such an article will surely be hard to dispose of profitably, for would not a possible buyer suspect it was stolen?"

"Unless he has a prospect already. Someone unconcerned as to legalities."

She frowned. "Yet he could ask for any amount, to the ruin of the estate, and would you not be willing to give it to ransom your daughter?"

"Without hesitation."

She kissed his cheek. "I knew it. But he has not asked this. Why?"

"I don't pretend to understand the mind of James Burke."

"It would seem the fifty thousand pounds should have been enough for anyone. Is there any possibility the kidnapper of last year is a different man?"

"We've compared the handwriting on both notes, and it is the same. There can be no doubting, for certain peculiarities are present in both."

"And yet I've heard of no renovations or additions at his estate; he does not drive a new carriage or dress extravagantly. Where has the money gone?" Dru rose to sit across from him on the settle. "Unless he spent it all on his plantation in Georgia."

"He's bought land in America, has he? That would account for expenditures, certainly." The earl shook his head in disgust. "He could have gamed it to the four winds for all we know, Druscilla, or tossed it into the sea. What does it matter? He has Clarissa."

"If he's not captured, though; if—when Rissa is returned, must we live constantly with the threat of his villainy?" She grew angry now and rejoiced in the return of her old friend. Anger left little room for drooping spirits. "Every time he has need of funds, will he capture one of us and demand payment?"

The earl's face suffused with colour. Closing the lid of the box, he set it aside and pushed himself to his feet. "He *must* be caught. 'Tis the only possible answer. But if the worst happens, and he is not apprehended, he'll no longer be able to dwell in England without fearing for his *own* capture. Now that he's allowed his identity to be discovered."

It was a point that troubled her more than any. Reluctant to cause her father further upset, she asked hesitantly, "Why do you suppose he was so thoughtless tonight, Papa? Using our own stationery . . . it is almost as though he doesn't care anymore."

The earl, weary of being questioned, stated he'd no idea and that he must see to ordering the carriage. There was still plenty of time before three, but he would order it in any case.

As he left the room, a sudden thought struck her. Duncan felt something had forced James to act in haste. She thought hurriedly of the dinner. Had anything occurred then to trigger him?

Her reverie was interrupted by the sound of voices in the hall. The surgeon was speaking to the earl, and she rushed to hear his evaluation.

"They'll both be fine, if allowed to rest," the doctor said, and tugged at his beard thoughtfully. "The viscount is concussed and shouldn't sleep, though do keep him quiet. Your footman has a number of bruises, which is to be expected after lying beneath a heavy wardrobe for several hours." His lip quirked upward at one corner. "I expect he'll spend a sore day or two. But someone needs to reassure the man. He's distressing himself mightily. Thinks he'll be sacked for this night's business. And, my lord, I must admit to a great curiosity. What goes on here?"

"You'll be told all," said Lord Cathburn, "but I must press upon you to stay. Your services could well be needed before the sun rises, and I wish for you to accompany me in the carriage."

The doctor was willing, but Dru exclaimed, "Are you not to go alone, Papa?"

"I'll stop the carriage before we get within sight of the harbour and ride Trumpet the remaining distance. Burke can have no objection to that, for he'll know Clarissa will need transportation when she is returned."

"Then I shall go, too," Dru said firmly.

"No, that you will not! There is nothing to be gained except danger to my other child."

"Rissa will need me when she is freed."

"Of course she will, but she'll have your comfort as soon as we arrive home."

"If you do not allow me to ride within the carriage, Papa," she said with a growing defiance, "I shall follow you on Cinnamon. And do not think of locking me within my room, for I will find a way out, and make your life miserable ever after!"

And she would, too, the doctor thought in shocked amusement as he looked from one angry face to the other. He had no doubt of the victor of *this* argument.

"I go as well," said Sebastian from the doorway of the library, his hand pressed against the doorframe for support. Alfred went to stand beside him uncertainly, but the viscount waved him away and walked unsteadily toward them. His face was a carefully composed mask and gave little hint, other than its lack of colour, as to the pain he must be feeling.

When he reached them, Dru took his arm and turned beseeching eyes toward her father. The earl puffed out his cheeks in exasperation. "Oh, very well!" he sighed. "Let us call the housekeeper, the maids, and several grooms while we are about it. Perhaps tiny Hildy Jessup would like to accompany us, too. Someone must go and ask her." And so saying, he went to speak with Hayes.

Dru gave the viscount a small smile of triumph and hurried up the stairs, explaining she meant to change her dress. But as she walked toward her room, she slowed her steps while recalling the earlier question concerning James.

She tried again to think about their conversation at dinner, and what might have spurred him to kidnap Rissa without troubling to conceal his identity. It seemed important to remember, but her thoughts were so jumbled she could hardly think.

She recollected making evident her sisterly feelings toward Sebastian. He and Rissa had become exuberant after that. They laughed over the smallest things, made the silliest jests and toasts, and generally behaved as foolishly as only young people in love could. Dru struggled to remember James's reaction to all of this. He had been very quiet, had he not? In truth, all three of them had become subdued; she because of her concern over Duncan; the earl perhaps because he mourned the loss of the viscount for herself; and James . . . why?

Dru's steps slowed to a halt, and she stared blindly at her bedroom door. She had posed a question about love, and he'd answered it with the sincerity of strongly felt emotion. Something about not being able to live without the loved one . . .

She pressed her fist to her stomach. The air seemed to fly from her lungs.

James had known. He saw the love between Rissa and Sebastian. The heavy, growing quiet of his demeanour, and the darkness of his countenance should have signaled them all. He had watched the two of them with jealous, hurting eyes. How could she not have seen?

James had never recovered from Rissa's rejection. He loved her still, or what passed for love in his mind. Rissa had been his object all along, and Dru had never been in danger; that was only a subterfuge. And now she knew as certainly as she had ever known anything what his intentions were.

James never meant to return to his estate. He had Rissa, and he did not plan to let her go.

Rissa's world had become a series of impressions. The sound of oars striking water. The damp touch of fog on her skin. The sting of salty breaths of air. The relentless persistence of his voice speaking words she could not understand and did not want to hear. And then: a rope descending, and herself linked within it to be pulled upward to the cries of rough voices and the touch of strong hands. And him again, leading her toward a small room. The door closing, and the comfort of a bed with clean linens.

She would sleep, if only he would go away.

"Please, Clarissa," James said gently. "Please speak to me. You know I will not harm you; I have told you repeatedly."

In the quietness of the room, soothed by the gentle rocking of the vessel, she felt her senses returning. Though she hardly trusted herself to speak—there seemed not enough air, and her breathing came in short gasps—she needed to understand, needed to make some order from the terrible events which had befallen her this night.

"You . . . will not . . . harm me?" she asked between breaths. "But . . . you already have."

Rissa heard him fall to his knees beside her bed. "It was an accident. A terrible, unforgivable accident. I would give you my eyes, if I could, and not regret it, save for the loss of seeing your incomparable face again."

"It was you? James . . . it was you?"

"Yes, I thought you knew," he said regretfully. "I assumed that was what you meant when you said I'd already hurt you."

She covered her face with her hands. "I meant Sebastian. When you struck him . . . you hurt me." She swallowed and gathered courage. "Did you . . . kill him?"

"No, my dear. I know you are fond of him, and besides, I'm not a murderer." With a harder edge in his voice he added, "He is fortunate I am not."

"Oh, James. Why have you done this?"

"Do not weep, dearest Clarissa," he entreated, and attempted to remove her hands from her face. At his touch she flinched away, and he quickly withdrew. When he spoke again, she heard bitterness. "Why? You ask me why? I should think it obvious. It is because I love you."

"You . . . love me?" Her lips curled scornfully. "This is how you behave toward those you love?"

She sensed a sudden coldness in him and knew a moment's fear when he rose from his knees. But after standing awhile beside her, he pulled a chair close to the bed and sat down.

"I shall tell you a story," he said quietly.

Rissa clutched at the bedding in a nervous paroxysm. The gentleness of his voice was so in variance to his actions, she found herself wanting to scream, or run away, if only she could.

"This story blames no one," he continued, "for we are all players upon a stage, as Shakespeare said. We act as we must, in reaction to our own circumstances. Does one blame the lion for making his kill? Or a less violent example: Can the leaf fail to fall from the tree? Yet blame could be made in this story I shall relate, were one so inclined, and the guilt would lie in several directions." He took a deep breath as though to calm himself. "But I make no accusations, for I am not innocent myself."

He paused as though waiting for her to comment on the indisputable truth of his final statement, but she remained silent. With a little smile he continued, "We must go back several years. Back to a time when a young man—let us call him the hero of the story, for want of a better term, and not meaning the word as a comment on any special merits in his character that are deserving of such a noble designation—back to a time when our hero was little more than a boy. This boy had a widowed mother who loved him very well, but who was discontented in many ways. Now whether the mother was discontented due to circumstance or a fault in her nature, the boy knew not. He was only aware that a pall of bitterness hung about her perpetually, though occasionally the vestiges of a brighter spirit broke through. Such moments were happy times for him, and he drank of them as one suffering from great thirst.

"One of the things which pleased the mother most was to visit the king's wife in the castle on the hill. Whenever she was issued an invitation to dine, or to call for tea, hours were spent in anticipation. Often the boy would be invited as well, and there he would walk and talk with the king's daughters, the two most beautiful princesses in the land. But the boy learned to dread these outings, for after the conclusion of each, his mother would repine in her chamber for days, and could not be comforted."

Rissa turned her face toward him, listening in spite of herself. She began to relax, lulled by the gentle sound of his words.

"Years passed in this manner," James said. "The mother died, as mothers always do. The boy went away to school and grew to manhood. Then he returned to his home.

"Many things had fallen into neglect during his absence, he realized. His estate had never been a castle like the king's, but it once held a form of glory. Now he saw broken furnishings, shabby appointments, holes in the roof, crumbling beams, tattered wallcoverings, smashed windows. Moreover, the livestock had been sold to provide for his education. It seemed a hopeless shambles, irredeemable, for there was no gold in his pockets. Even the peasants had forsaken his lands and stolen what they might, excepting the faithful housekeeper, who had served his mother and himself for many years.

"He might have left then and abandoned all for the great City, where he could earn his bread as none of his forebears had done in centuries. Some lowly clerk's position could have been his, had not Providence intervened in the sickness of his housekeeper. It was a sickness unto death, and he could not forsake her to the ministrations of strangers. So he stayed and nursed her through the months of her dying."

"I never knew you did that," Rissa interrupted.

"I didn't want anyone to know," he said softly. "But back to our story. The housekeeper lay dying. Suddenly she began to relate the most astounding revelation which could be imagined. She could not leave this earth without his knowing, she said, though his mother had never intended it. But her conscience would not let her go cleanly to her Maker did she not tell all. So tell him she did."

He gave a short laugh. "Imagine our hero's state of mind when he heard he was not the son of his mother's husband, but of her lover. It is never a pleasant thing to know one is illegitimate. But to learn that one's father was once the king!"

Rissa jerked in shock, and he lay a soothing hand on her arm. "No, not the present king, but his elder brother, who was slain by a jealous husband for his unlawfully amorous nature."

"Was it your father who—"

"No, Clarissa. Richard Burke had little energy and less courage. I suppose you were too young to know him well before he died. But on with the story—"

"No, James. No more stories. Just tell me as it happened."

He seemed pleased. "Very well. When I learned your Uncle Edmond was my father, my first inclination was to tell the present earl. But then I realized it could be of little use. Had Edmond married my mother, the Hall would have been mine. But by-blows have no rights, as you know. So I was entitled to nothing.

"But it came to me how I might achieve my inheritance, or at least some portion it."

"Marriage," Rissa said. She sat up and pulled her knees beneath her. His actions, though unforgivable, were becoming easier to understand, and she must be on her guard or she would feel sorry for him. And if she ever expressed such a thing to Dru, her sister might never speak to her again.

"Marriage," he agreed. "To one of you. And such was the state of my feelings at the time that I didn't care which. But when I renewed my acquaintance with your family, a peculiar thing happened." Though his tone became flippant, she sensed the depth of his feelings as he added, "I fell quite desperately in love with you."

The chair creaked as he leaned back. "Perhaps I didn't allow you enough time to love me as well, but you were destined for a London Season. I couldn't let you go without asking for your hand. Too many gentleman awaited the sweetness of your smiles there; gentlemen far more eligible than I. I knew it was too soon, but I asked you anyway, and of course you refused. The rejection made me angry at first, for I thought: had Edmond done the proper thing, had he married my mother instead of leaving her in a desperate situation, you would not have refused your wealthy and titled cousin.

"So I went home, my spirits crushed. Everywhere about me was ruin. My legal sire's estate was crumbling to dust, just as my own life was in ashes. None of it meant anything to me anymore.

"And then a plan began to form in my mind. A plan which included the attainment of a reasonable portion of my true father's estate. A plan which included you.

"You know the rest, and how terribly I botched everything. I didn't realize until we reached my rooms how seriously wounded you'd been. Had all gone as I wished, we'd have spent the last year together in happiness. But when I realized you were blind, and so terrorized I hardly knew you, I was fearful for your safety; fearful that you would not return to sanity unless restored to your family. So I disguised my voice and determined to await another day to claim your love, and in the meantime use the funds to begin my own establishment—our home, Clarissa. And this I have done."

Rissa heard a roaring in her ears. Her temples pounded warningly. "You . . . never meant to return me when the ransom was paid?"

"No, my dear," he said with chilling simplicity. "Do not think me cruel. I knew you would come to love me in time. Just as I know you will soon love me now. When we are wed—when you are under my protection and legal guardianship, I shall teach you to love me.

"Have I not prepared well? My ship has been readied for this moment for weeks, and though I hoped to win your heart and make this elopement unnecessary, all shall be right eventually.

"We await only the arrival of your father with the tiara. He thinks I will release you upon its delivery, poor man. I have no wish to hurt him, but the tiara is rightfully mine, you know. And yours. You shall wear it at our wedding."

"James . . ." she pleaded. "I do not love you. I love Sebastian."

He pressed his fingers to her lips. "Never say his name in my presence again, Clarissa. I will not be responsible."

She pushed his fingers away. "They will find us!" she cried. "Dru will remember about your land in America. Papa will follow you all the way there, if need be."

"They will search in vain. I purposely lied that day. Though I did first sail to America, I went next to Australia and purchased my land. And if ever they find us there, we'll have long been married. What can they do then?"

Rissa turned her back to him and covered her ears. James stroked her hair, then began to remove her hairpins. She lay unmoving beneath his hands, her body stiff in outrage.

"Don't worry, my darling," he said. "I shall not harm you. Your hair has become mussed from our ride on horseback. I shall have to assist you until we find a proper maid, though I have no talent in styles. You must be content with simplicity for awhile."

To her horror he removed a hairbrush from a drawer and began to pull it through her hair in long, slow strokes. "Such beautiful hair, Clarissa," he whispered. "It is softer than silk."

Lord Cathburn opened the door of the carriage and stepped out. " 'Tis good the fog is so thick," he said to his companions. "But remember how well it carries sound and keep your voices down."

The other three passengers alighted from the carriage. Dru held the tiara within its box while the earl mounted Trumpet, then she handed it to him.

"Be careful, Papa," she whispered.

"I shall. But you should get within the carriage. 'Twill ease my mind. Who knows whether Burke's men lay hidden about?"

"Don't worry about me. I'll be safe." *Because James has no interest in me,* she added silently. *He only means to have the tiara and sail away with Rissa.* But she knew better than to tell her father, for what rash action might he take then? If he believed her suspicions at all.

There was only one man with whom she intended to share her knowledge. Duncan would know what to do. If only she could find him.

Lord Cathburn gave them a salute and prodded Trumpet to a canter. Within seconds he was invisible to them, though the sounds of pounding hooves continued for some time before fading away.

The mist drifted in patches like wraiths searching for a resting place; every little hollow of land beckoned and held quantities of the billowing stuff. Combined with darkness, it was an excellent veil to cloak her wanderings. But first she must escape the escort of Sebastian and the doctor.

"You are looking very frail, Lord Sebastian," she

said, comforting herself with the knowledge it was true. "Why do you not lie within the carriage?"

He did not remove his eyes from the direction of the harbour. "I'd rather be with your father," he said feelingly.

"I am certain of it. But it's impossible."

"I know you have told me of Burke's commands, but with the fog it's doubtful he could see the shore at all from his ship."

Dr. Aaron said, "The young lady's right, though. You need the rest, and we may as well all sit within." He put his hand under the viscount's elbow and guided him toward the coach. Dru made as if to follow, then gave a little cry of pain.

"Are you all right?" the doctor asked.

"Oh! Yes, it's only a spasm in my foot. Do you go inside; I shall walk it out for a few moments. Don't worry; I'll not go far."

He acquiesced, and she stumbled off bravely. As soon as the carriage was out of sight, she began to run toward the harbour.

Dru soon had cause to be thankful for her daily walks, for otherwise she could not have continued to run for such a long time. Even so, the run quickly became painful, but she persisted. By the time she reached the village, however, her breaths were coming in short spurts, and she had to slow her pace or drop.

The little shops were insubstantial within their wispy shrouds, like dream fragments bordered in black. She turned her head from side to side, watching not for James's men, but something more sinister; something she could not name. But nothing disturbed her, and, scolding herself as an excitable goose, she continued on.

The road took a sharp downturning now as she approached the harbour. She reckoned her run had been nearly ten minutes in duration. Would her father already

be rowing the boat toward the unseen ship? Or would he
see her and order her back to the carriage?

A breath of wind scattered the fog into smaller rem-
nants, and she was startled to see what must be James's
ship floating in plain view some distance offshore.
Quickly she hid behind a stack of rowboats. She looked
about her tensely, hoping to catch a glimpse of Duncan
or one of his men. She saw only boats and fishermen's
gear. And yes, there was her father, just now launching
the rowboat. Then the mist dropped, and he was hidden
from view.

She began to dart from one boat, or stack of boats, to
another. There was no sign of anyone. The entire harbour looked to be uninhabited, as though these relics of
man were ancient castoffs of a lost civilization. She did
not dare even whisper Duncan's name, fearing someone
would hear her on the ship. But he wasn't here anyway,
was he? Unless he hid among the outcropping of rocks
that edged either end of the inlet. But those were too far
away and looked impossibly hard to climb.

"That's far enough!" she heard James call. "Swim
ashore, Lord Cathburn!" Despite the revulsion she felt
in hearing him, she shook her head in perplexity. One
would never imagine that a villain like him could possess such a patient, kind voice, even raised as it was to
project across the water.

She strained her eyes but could see nothing beyond a
few feet of shore. And then her father said, "Let Rissa
appear before I abandon the tiara. Row her toward me
at least."

Good for you, Papa! she thought. But James only
laughed and said, "Do not attempt to manipulate me,
my lord! If all is not done as I ask, we shall sail away
before dawn brings the fishermen! Is the tiara worth that
much to you?"

"No!" Lord Cathburn said dejectedly. "It is not. The

tiara is here, and I leave the boat as you ask." There came a splashing sound, then the smaller noise of swimming. Unlike many men who spend much of their lives on ships, the earl was an expert swimmer; he had even taught his daughters to swim, judging the skill an important one to the inhabitants of an island, albeit a big one.

Dru knew a fearful sinking of spirits. Until this point she had hopes of finding Duncan and telling him of her conviction concerning James's plans. But even if she found him now, there was little he could do except commission a boat and attempt to follow. And every moment of such an enterprise would be fraught with danger for both Rissa and Duncan.

She berated herself for not telling her father when she had the opportunity. But what could he have done?

Dru bowed her head, the heaviness of her grief not even allowing of tears. There was no comfort now, excepting the hope she had been wrong. Would that Rissa was being rowed toward shore at this very moment.

Then the fog parted like a curtain before a play, and she saw not Rissa, but a man climbing the ship's ladder, the mahogany box clutched closely to his chest. Within a moment he was aboard, abandoning the rowboat to find its own path among the waves. She saw James—it must be James, for he was the only man among them dressed like a gentleman—open the box, then hold the tiara high above his head in a gesture of victory.

"It is more beautiful than I dreamed!" he shouted. "I thank you, Lord Cathburn!"

The earl dragged himself from the water and turned to face the ship. "Send me my daughter, Burke!" he cried.

"I'm sorry, my uncle," James called. He paused, as though waiting for a reaction to this unexpected title, but the earl was too dumbfounded to speak. "I must take Clarissa with me," he went on. "We are to be wed! Do not fear for her; I mean to take tender care of her! And now, farewell!"

"No!" screamed Lord Cathburn.

Dru ran to him then, for what did it matter if she were seen now? She threw her arms about him, and he wept as freely as she did herself. Never in her life had she known such sorrow; not the death of her mother, not even the first kidnapping of Rissa, for then there had been hope.

Unwilling to miss her last link with her dear sister, even such an unsatisfactory one as this, she turned her gaze back to the ship. Its contours were hazy and shimmering through a wall of tears. And then, gradually, disbelieving at first, and finally unable to deny it longer, she saw that something was terribly, dreadfully wrong.

"Papa," she whispered in panicked tones.

The earl rubbed tears from his eyes and looked at her, then the ship. With a heartbreaking groan he sank to the rocky beach and covered his eyes with his hands.

The vessel was on fire.

10

The fire was burning in several parts of the ship. Angry, startled shouts turned fearful as the men scurried frantically, trying to stamp out flames, throwing feeble buckets of water upon thirsty tongues of fire. It soon became apparent their efforts could not succeed.

Lord Cathburn rushed to his feet and into the water.

"Where are you going?" Dru cried.

"I shall find her and save her!"

"You cannot, Papa!" she wailed. "You won't make it in time!"

"I won't if I do not try!"

"I cannot lose you as well!" she pleaded. But he swam on.

One of the sailors jumped ship, his back glowing in flames. Dru closed her eyes and wished she could hide her ears from the sound of his screams.

More men began to jump into the water to swim for shore, though some floundered, having not the skill. A few grabbed onto the rowboat and pulled themselves in, helping others as they might. A lifeboat fell from the ship, and more men clasped onto it.

Dru looked to see who had loosened the lifeboat from its moorings, but the brilliance of the fire against the night sky made vision difficult. The man standing by the rail was tall enough to be Duncan, but that was ridiculous. How could he be on the ship?

She cupped her hands about her eyes and squinted. Gradually she became aware that others joined her. From the rocky cliffs, from inside boats, Duncan's men came to stand on the shore. Every man of them had a weapon, whether sword, pistol, or stick, and they spaced themselves out like sentinels awaiting the onslaught. But Duncan was not among them.

Before long, the sailors began to arrive at the beach. None of them had the strength or heart to fight, and they lay themselves down in docile rows on the sand, as ordered. A couple of Duncan's men walked from one prisoner to the other, tying their hands.

Sebastian and Dr. Aaron ran toward her from the road. "What is happening, Dru?" the viscount exclaimed. "Can you account it? The carriage's axle has broken! We saw the fire and came as quickly as we could! Where is Rissa?"

Dru looked at him with devastated eyes and shook her head. She walked to him and put her arms about his waist, burying her face against his chest. Looking wildly at the ship, he returned her embrace, but shook his head repeatedly.

"No, no, it cannot be!"

"I shall never be happy again," she sobbed.

"Rissa!" he cried, his arms loosening. "My beautiful Rissa!"

Dru frowned and tried to hold him tighter. From the sound of his voice, he grew hysterical, and it would not help his head any. "I know, Sebastian," she soothed. "But you must try to be brave. You will become ill."

"No, you don't understand!" The viscount removed her hands from his waist and set her aside, laughing delightedly. "It's Rissa! She's all right!" And he plunged into the foam.

Dru looked after him in disbelief, then dawning ecstasy. It *was* Rissa! She swam valiantly toward them, the earl and Doug Harris swimming by her side. Dru cried happily and ran into the water.

The earl's elder daughter was to find the last yards of her swim the most difficult, for one can hardly make progress when being held by loved ones who thought you dead. The earl soon found himself in the same pleasant predicament. But at last they all reached the shore and collapsed into a laughing, relieved, sodden heap.

Dru held one of Rissa's hands while Sebastian held the other. The earl had to be content with watching, but he told himself he didn't mind. Something about the way the viscount looked at Rissa was making him feel hopeful again. Though he didn't understand how the boy could change allegiance so quickly. Hopefully he was not the wandering sort.

Dru kissed her sister's hand and said, "You were so brave! Swimming all that way!"

"Mr. Harris guided me the whole distance," Rissa said, her face serene.

"Rissa . . ." Dru said admiringly, "how you can be so calm, after your experience! I can't understand it."

"I was not so calm awhile ago when Duncan and Harris opened the door to my cabin and told me to prepare to swim or be towed through the water! But the thought of escaping restored me. And Duncan did not start the fires until I was in the sea, so I had not that danger. I swam slowly, though; I could hear the men rushing past me, but Harris said we must not get on one of the boats because they might try to use me as a shield when they reached land. So we swam on!"

Dru had hardly heard anything past the first sentence. "Duncan was on the ship?" she asked.

"Yes. He was responsible for my rescue. Harris told

me that he and Duncan used the fog's cover to swim to the ship shortly after James and I arrived, and they stayed in the vessel's shadow until Papa delivered the tiara. Imagine! All that time in the water. Then, when everyone's attention was captured by James and Papa, Duncan and Harris climbed the anchor's moorings and came aboard.

"They searched for me, and when I was found, Duncan ordered Harris to accompany me back. They lowered me down the far side of the ship with a rope, and we hid in the channel until Duncan set the fires and the men were distracted."

"But . . . where is Duncan now?" Dru asked, remembering the tall figure on the burning ship.

Rissa's face became grave. "Is he not here?"

Dru got to her feet. There was no sign of Duncan, though many people were moving about. Dr. Aaron was checking the captives for injuries; Duncan's men were searching for more survivors, and now the villagers had begun to appear. Several of them walked around dispensing blankets, and one or two ladies served steaming mugs of tea. As she watched, one of them came in their direction and supplied hot beverages. Dru refused her drink, for if Duncan could not have one, she would not partake either.

Then Crickley ran toward them carrying blankets from the carriage. He even brought his overcoat, and they wrapped it about Rissa's shoulders.

Among the bedlam, hoarse cries were heard; seeing the gestures of the crowd, they turned toward the ship. The vessel was now totally engulfed in flames, and it cracked and popped and groaned in protest. With a terrible grace, it folded toward the water like a great, dying beast. And then it began to sink.

The crowd sighed as the water closed over the last of

the flaming timber. It had been a fine ship, and the death of beauty is never easily borne.

Dru watched with stinging eyes. She had been through so many emotional exchanges this evening, she could not react more. Her heart had turned to stone.

Dr. Aaron ran to join them. "The captain of the vessel says all have made it ashore, excepting their master. It's a wonder there weren't more injuries. Only one man is seriously hurt, with burns to his back; a few others have burnt hands, and one has an arm fracture."

"What of Duncan?" Dru asked woodenly.

"I've heard the earl's men mention him. They continue to search."

" 'Twould be a pity do they not find him," Lord Cathburn said. "He's a fine fellow, and we have him to thank for Clarissa's life."

Dru looked at her father with expressionless eyes. He seemed genuinely sorry, but it was a sorrow which could not long weigh his spirits, for his daughter was free.

No one knew what she was feeling. Not to anyone had she mentioned her growing affection for Duncan. But that was because she'd spent so much time voicing her suspicions and silly ideas about him. It was only yesterday that she'd come to realize she loved him. Now she would pay the penalty. If Duncan was dead, she would bear the pain alone. For how could anyone understand the depth of her loss?

Even Rissa could be of little comfort; to look at her now was to see happiness in the flesh. She almost glowed. It was a well-deserved happiness, too, and Dru would not be the one to destroy it.

"What shall we do with the prisoners?" Dr. Aaron asked. "You're the magistrate, after all."

"Yes, but I've no dungeons to spare," the earl returned. "Have the men house 'em in the gatehouse to-night and guard 'em well. Tomorrow we'll see."

"The captain swears they didn't know Burke was doing anything unlawful."

"Well, that's what I'd expect him to say, though mayhap he tells the truth. I've little desire to punish working sailors; I'll probably let the scoundrels off after scaring 'em a bit. It's Burke I want. I'd like to see his brown-haired head on a platter."

"Brown-haired!" Sebastian looked at Dru, his eyes wide. "I have just thought! Miss Lumquist's prediction!"

"But she told *Dru* to beware the deep water," Rissa said. "I believe she'd have done better to tell *me.*"

"She's never gotten anything exactly right," Dru said faintly.

"Miss Lumquist's a shocker, and that's the truth," the earl said cheerfully. "But what about Burke, doctor? D'you suppose he went down with the ship?"

"I daresay. Probably they'll find his body washed ashore within the next days, unless he was pinned beneath heavy wreckage."

"Papa," Rissa said slowly. "He was not as evil as we thought. Only misguided."

"I cannot believe my ears," said Lord Cathburn.

"He was Uncle Edmond's son, Papa; your nephew. He felt the ransom was due him as his rightful portion."

"Ha! Well, I'm surprised to know it, but glad that all Edmond's offspring don't feel that way."

"What do you mean?"

"Well . . . guess you're old enough to know, though I don't want to sully your tender ears with such stuff. Fact is, you've cousins all over this shire."

Dru and Rissa absorbed the information in silence. A moment later, Rissa said, "That may well be. I don't think James knew it, though. His worst fault was thinking he loved me. He planned all along to marry me, whether I wanted to or not. Even last year, when he first kidnapped me. My—illness frightened him, however; that's why he released me."

"If he had not—if you had not become blind," Dru said wonderingly, "you might have been lost to us forever."

Rissa quietly agreed.

Sebastian placed his arm about Rissa's shoulders. "But that was not meant to happen," he said heartily. Now that he was near Rissa, his head no longer seemed to bother him, Dru noted, not without fondness despite her pain. "She was meant for me. Which leads to an entirely inappropriate question, Lord Cathburn, but one I am unable to delay a moment longer. I would like to ask for Lady Rissa's hand in marriage."

Lord Cathburn looked at him in astonishment. His gaze moved from the viscount's face to his elder daughter's. He could find no objections there. Dru didn't appear hurt by it, either. She didn't even look to be listening. Joy spread across his heart like a healing balm. *Mrs. Tweetle, here I come!* he thought.

With much harumphing and false reluctance, he gave his consent.

While the blissful couple embraced, oblivious to the crowd around them, several cries were heard. "Someone comes!" said a woman's voice. "Another survivor!"

Dru and the others turned and walked slowly toward the sea. She stood in front, her hands pressed tightly together. Someone did swim toward shore, but, even though dawn now illumined the sky, she could not determine his identity. The swimmer was dreadfully weary and lifted his head for air at suffocating intervals, allowing only the briefest glimpses of a pale face beneath wet, dark hair.

Was it Duncan? Or was it James?

At last the survivor reached the shallows and knelt in exhaustion, his hands upon his knees. Dru waded toward him, her feet leaden with dread, her heart not daring to hope. And then she was close enough to recognize him.

"Duncan!" she cried ecstatically.

While she continued to approach, several men rushed forward to assist him, hiding him from view. Still, he looked around their shoulders and gave her a brief smile. But his gaze met hers an instant only before turning toward the prisoners lying on the beach. Even at this distance, Dru saw the bleak, hollow look in his eyes and shivered.

She wanted to run and fling her arms around him. He looked in need of comfort, and she needed the reassurance that he was truly all right. But something in his manner warned her off, and she stood uncertainly, the water foaming coldly about her knees, until the earl demanded she return to shore.

It was a tired but comfortable group that met around the earl's table a few hours later. The carriage's broken axle had caused them to wait until a second conveyance could be brought from the Hall, and they had been home only long enough to wash the salt water from their skin and change into dry clothing.

Now Hayes and Jessup served their plates with the chef's finest breakfast offerings. Thanks to the earl's being present when a trawler pulled into port that morning, there were even smoked herring and oysters fresh from the sea. Lord Cathburn and Sebastian fell upon the food like hungry dogs.

Rissa had a healthy appetite, too, Dru noticed; it was as though the last twenty-four hours had never occurred. She felt awed by her sister's reaction. Last year Rissa had fallen to pieces and never fully regained the serenity that had previously been so much a part of her character. Now she looked to be recapturing her former poise.

Of course this time Rissa had not had to adjust to blindness. Nevertheless, she'd endured capture and the threat of estrangement from her loved ones forever; she'd swum a great distance in total darkness. Not many could tolerate such events and sit down to a full plate mere hours later. What had caused the difference? Was it love? Dru could not help putting the question to her.

"Love helps," Rissa replied, and leaned her head in the viscount's direction. In answer he squeezed her hand, then returned with unromantic haste to his food. "But even more, I think my most overwhelming feeling is one of relief."

"You mean you're relieved because it's over, and everything turned out happily? It is that which causes your relaxation?"

"Well . . ." The light dimmed in her eyes. "Everything did not turn out happily for James. No, you must not scold me for having sympathy for him, Dru. He never intended to harm me. And yes, naturally I am relieved that it's over. But I mean something more as well."

She placed her fork beside her plate and leaned back. "When I was kidnapped last spring, the fright was the greater because I didn't know the identity of my assailant. If I could be abducted in front of my own house, it seemed to me I could be secure nowhere. Now that I know it was James and that he had a reason for his actions—no matter how much in error his reasoning was—the world seems sane again. I feel . . . safe."

Sebastian swallowed a bite of egg and said, "I hope you will always feel safe with me."

Lord Cathburn pointed at Dru's plate. "Eat, child.

You can't retire to bed without something in your stomach."

Dru stirred her food in a gesture of compliance, but she could not eat. It was a curious feeling to be hungry but to have no appetite. And there could be no doubting why she felt so.

Unable to bear it longer, she said, "Where's Duncan, Papa? I thought you'd invited him to breakfast."

"So I did, Druscilla. He'd best hurry or they'll be naught left. Especially with the way my future son is attacking Andre's cuisine!" He laughed merrily and thought, *Future son!* Wait until Mrs. Tweetle hears!

At that moment he decided there'd be no sleep for him that day. A certain lady would be asked a long-withheld question, and if he received the answer he expected, the remaining hours would be spent making plans. For why should they delay any longer? Time was passing every minute! Time that should be spent together.

"Excuse me," Hayes said. "Someone is knocking at the front door." He bowed and exited.

Someone was indeed knocking; the sound was growing in persistence and urgency by the second. By the time Hayes reached the door, the small group at the breakfast table had grown silent, their ears attuned to hear the identity of such a demanding caller.

"Who are *you?*" they heard Hayes say disdainfully. "And why have you come to the front? Whatever business you have must be conducted at the servants' entrance."

"I've got to see the lord!" said a high, clear voice. "Right now, mister! Let me see 'im, please!"

"The earl is dining at present and cannot be bothered by a raggedy, dirt-faced urchin like you."

The child gave a grunt of frustration. "Who are you to be callin' me names?" he demanded. "You with yer nose like a hawk's beak and hairy ears, too! I smelled yer feet three leagues afore I got here!"

"Oh, my!" Rissa whispered, giggling into her napkin.

"I must see this creature," Lord Cathburn grinned. But before he reached the doorway, sounds of a scuffle were heard, then a crash. Rushing into the hall, they found Hayes and a boy lying on the floor; the butler was clutching desperately at the child's flailing ankles.

The boy looked angrily back at his pursuer. "If you made me break it," he cried, "the lord will 'ang you from 'is roof by yer toenails!"

Lord Cathburn saw the mahogany box gripped beneath the captive's arm and grew very still. "What have you there, boy?" he demanded.

The child whipped his head around and smiled widely. He removed an unspeakable cap and made a semblance of a bow, a difficult enterprise while lying on the floor. "If 'ee'll let me go," he said, "I'll show you, sir."

"Let him go, Hayes," the earl said evenly.

Hayes released him and stood up. With great dignity he straightened his jacket, positioned himself against the wall, crossed his arms over his chest, and fixed his haughty, indifferent eyes upon the handrail.

The child was on his feet in an instant. He gave the butler an insolent look, then turned to Lord Cathburn with an angelic expression. "Me name's Bradley, good sir," he said humbly. "And I've come to give you wot I think belongs to you. Found it on the shore, I did; washed up after everyone 'ad gone 'ome."

Lord Cathburn accepted the box with trembling fingers. He took a deep breath, closed his eyes momentarily, and lifted the lid.

Sealed within the protective wood and velvet lining, the tiara had suffered no damage during its brief sojourn in the sea. The earl expelled air from his lungs in a relieved sigh. Dru and Sebastian murmured in admiration. Seeing Rissa's attentive, inquiring face, Lord Cathburn removed the tiara and placed it in her hands; when she'd explored its surface briefly, he placed it upon her hair with tender reverence.

"You shall wear it soon, my dear," he said, and stood back to admire her.

Dru's eyes began to fill. "You look like a princess," she said.

"That you do," said Sebastian, and kissed her cheek.

"She do!" Bradley affirmed. "A princess in a story!"

"And as for you, young man," said Lord Cathburn, "who are your parents?"

"'Adn't got any. Just been livin' along the coast. Came all the way from Lonnon, I did. Been walkin' since winter."

"Is that so?" He looked him up and down. "Would you like a job?"

Bradley tilted his head and gave him a speculative stare. "Doin' wot, sir?"

"Oh, stableboy at first. Then, depending on how you do, anything could happen. If you stay around 'till you're older, you'll receive a goodly reward for your actions today."

The boy's eyes sparkled brightly. "Reward? Could we just skip o'er the stableboy part and get straight to the reward?"

Lord Cathburn grunted. "Can't do it. Someone'd knock a child like you over the head and steal it, and I'll not have that worry on my conscience."

Bradley puffed out his chest. "Nobody'd knock *me* on the 'ead. I'd stick me knoif in 'im and twirl 'im around like a windmill!"

"That's as may be, but if you want five hundred pounds, you'll stay five years."

"Five . . . 'unnert . . . pounds?" Bradley's eyes widened. Then he gave a piercing shout of joy that brought Jessup running in alarm. "Thank you, sir!" The boy knelt and kissed the earl's hand. "Thank you!"

Touched, Lord Cathburn said, "Thank *you*, Bradley."

Robert Hayes looked at the ceiling and chewed his tongue.

The earl tousled the child's hair. "Now get you off with the butler, boy. Hayes, take Bradley to the house-keeper and get him some decent clothes. Tell him how to get on."

Without visible emotion, Hayes did as he was told. The boy slapped the butler's arm companionably and gave him an impish grin while being led toward the kitchens.

Dru and the others exchanged smiles while the earl replaced the tiara in its box. They started to return to the dining room, but hesitated upon hearing a masculine tread on the stairs.

"Was that the tiara?" Duncan asked quietly. "Has the tiara been returned?"

"Duncan!" Lord Cathburn exclaimed. "Good to see you, and in proper clothing, too! Yes, 'twas the tiara. A young boy found it on the shore."

Dru felt her face flush. Her eyes did not know where to rest. She looked at Duncan nervously, then away and back again. Never had she felt so shy in her life, but never had she seen such a handsome man.

His thick, auburn hair was combed to elegant perfection; he wore a golden tan jacket of almost the same colour as his hair, a chamois-yellow waistcoat, white linen shirt and cravat, buckskin breeches, and boots with brown tops. He was dressed almost entirely in shades of brown, she realized. Why had she once thought brown a dull colour? On him it was vital, plush, rich.

Mayhap Miss Lumquist *had* meant herself when she

dreamt her vision. This brown-haired man *was* leading her into deep waters.

"Come have breakfast, Duncan," her father said.

"Thank you, no, Lord Cathburn. My men will be waiting for me to travel with them within moments. But I wish to speak with you, so I'll have a cup of coffee while you eat."

They re-entered the dining parlour and sat down. Jessup poured the investigator's coffee and refilled the other beverages. Dru watched Duncan without restraint now, her startled eyes large with hurt. Did he mean to leave without talking to her?

Duncan wrapped his hands about the coffee cup. He stared into the steaming liquid as though searching for something, then looked directly at the earl.

He does not look at me, Dru thought, her heart fluttering. *Why will he not look at me?*

"So you leave us already, Duncan?" asked Lord Cathburn. "Won't you stay and visit with us awhile? I'd be pleased to have you as guest instead of footman. Though you made a tolerable one. Don't you think so, Jessup?"

Jessup didn't know what to think about Duncan. In the last twenty-four hours the man had changed from a footman to a kidnapper to an investigator to a lord. It was too much for Jessup, especially with these pounding rocks in his head, the result of hours of "celebrating" the arrival of his twins.

Four females in his house, by all the tea in China. He lived in a house of women now.

But the earl was looking at him expectantly, and he gave a deferential bow. "Yes, my lord," he said. "He were a fine footman."

"And an even finer investigator," said Lord Cathburn. "Without him we'd have lost Rissa, there's no doubting.

Duncan, you can name your fee. We shall ever be in your debt."

Such gratitude obviously embarrassed the baron. He shifted uncomfortably and said, "The agreed-upon amount will be sufficient, my lord. I'm not as pleased as I'd have liked."

"Why not?" Sebastian asked in surprise. "There could not have been a better outcome."

Duncan's eyebrow lifted. "I should have gone to James's house as soon as the information was given me concerning the discrepancy in his sailing dates. It was an error on my part."

"But you'd have had no real proof," the earl demurred.

"Surely I could have found a sample of his handwriting there. It would've been something."

"Aw, you could speculate forever. I'll tell you this: Things would have been better all the way around had James not lost his head over Rissa. Now *that* would have made a better outcome. Let the blame fall where it truly should, Kyle."

Duncan looked into his cup and shook his head.

Dru felt his sadness. Maybe *this* was why he refused to glance in her direction. He was too upset. Rissa seemed to feel his despair, too. Hesitantly she asked, "After Harris and I left, did you see James?"

"I did." Duncan drained his coffee and waved away Jessup's efforts to pour him a second cup. "When he saw the fire, he ran immediately to your cabin, intent upon rescuing you, I'm certain. I was running about the deck trying to blend in with the other men, hoping to do what I could to prevent deaths. I saw him emerge from your room and start to search others; he must have thought you'd run away in his absence. I realized then that he'd continue to look until he burned, so I approached him and told him what I'd done.

"He looked at me in puzzlement, as though he didn't understand. I believe he didn't recollect ever seeing me before. I suppose he couldn't have been more surprised had the captain's wheel detached itself and rolled him down. Which was confirmation, my lord, that servants go largely unnoticed."

And then his eyes did flicker ever-so-briefly in her direction, and Dru caught her breath. *He is angry with me,* she thought. *That is why he won't meet my gaze. He's not forgiven me for my prejudice.*

"After the first bewilderment, he became enraged," Duncan continued. "I thought he meant to fight me, but then he seemed to become aware of the disaster around him and the hopelessness of it all. He asked me if I were certain you were all right, Lady Rissa. When I re-assured him, he clutched the tiara tightly to his chest and fled down the stairs of the ship.

"I called after him, for fleeing into the bowels of the vessel meant certain death. But he ran on, heedless to my cries. I started to run after him, but the ship began breaking up, and I went over the rail instead."

" 'Tis what you should've done, Duncan. Burke chose his own fate, and 'twas an easier one than he deserved."

"I don't know. I swam about for a long while, hoping to see if he survived. But never was there a sign of him. Yet, since the tiara's been found, I'm curious. It should've been caught among the ruins at the bottom, given James's last direction. Now I'm wondering if he had time to return updeck and throw it toward shore. If he did, maybe he meant it as an act of contrition. I hope so."

"You don't think—he couldn't have survived, could he?" Rissa said slowly. "Not that I want him dead; I don't, but . . ."

"No, Lady Clarissa. I can't believe there's any possibility he lives." The faint lines around Duncan's mouth deepened. "Well," he said, and pushed his chair away from the table, "I hear the sound of horses outside, so I'll be taking my leave of your fine family, Lord Cathburn."

"I'm sorry to see you go," the earl said. They all rose and accompanied the investigator to the outside, Dru's heart hammering the whole time. Would she not be granted even a moment to explain herself? How could this be happening?

Duncan shook the hands of Lord Cathburn and Sebastian. He kissed Rissa's hand, and she kissed his cheek, whispering her thanks. Then he stood before Dru, and she saw with what reluctance he lifted her hand to his lips and knew he would not have done so had he not already kissed her sister's.

"Duncan," Dru entreated between clenched teeth, her eyes beseeching him. But he kept his gaze riveted to her left shoulder and pretended not to hear. In a moment he was gone, sparing only a final wave for them all when he rode past the gate.

"A fine fellow," the earl said heartily.

"The very best," Sebastian agreed. "I hope to see him again someday."

Rissa said, "He has been kindness itself to me since I've known him. I have much to thank him for. Papa, you were brilliant to have hired him."

"Excuse me," Dru said, her voice breaking. And, rushing past their startled faces, she ran inside toward the sanctuary and seclusion of her room.

11

The next few days were intensely painful for Dru. Not only did she bear the loss of Duncan's esteem and apparently his love, but she forced herself to act as though nothing was wrong. It was a formidable task she set for herself; her feelings of hurt could be disguised but not hidden. Thus her efforts led to a certain stiffness of manner which her sister could not fail to notice.

"Dru, I must ask a question," Rissa said nervously one morning as they sat in the parlour awaiting Sebastian's arrival. They were alone, for Lord Cathburn spent the day with Mrs. Tweetle, an action which had become more frequent since the announcement of the older couple's betrothal.

"What question?" Dru answered distractedly as she paged through a lady's magazine. She was not interested in the magazine, but it gave her hands something to do. She certainly could not concentrate on embroidery or watercolours or practicing or anything else that might require the exertion of the mind, but she must appear to be occupied. So she turned the pages, and looked at pictures and words with no more comprehension than she could give Egyptian hieroglyphics.

Rissa said, "Do not become angry, but . . . you have seemed distant of late, and I'm wondering if you truly are happy for Sebastian and me. No, I'm saying it wrong! What I mean is . . . are you *certain* your affections do not lie in that quarter?" Before Dru could speak she continued bravely, her voice shaking, "Because if they . . . if you love Sebastian, I . . . I cannot, I *shall* not hurt you in this manner."

Dru set the magazine aside. "You would sacrifice Sebastian for me?"

Rissa's eyes began to look glassy. "Y-yes, I would. If you truly loved him, and if our marriage would give you pain."

"Shame on you, then," Dru said irritably. "Have you learned nothing from Jane Austen and Fanny Burney? The course of love is never supposed to run smoothly. If there is no opposition, then love becomes saccharine, bland, and dull. And where is the interest in that?"

Seeing Rissa's chin tremble, Dru repented and went to sit beside her. "Oh, dearest, pay no attention to me. I am only saying that you should be true to your heart, no matter what I feel. And how could you choose to hurt Sebastian over me, anyway? Two of you would be hurt instead of one, and none of that would make him love me. But do not despair! None of this is pertinent, because I don't love him. Well, I do, but only as a brother, as I've said before. So love him, marry him, and go with my blessing!"

Dru's forced gaiety struck falsely in Rissa's ears. With a confused look she said, "I know I'm not wrong about one thing. You may not be pining away for Sebastian, but *something* is troubling you. Dru, we have always shared everything. Will you not tell me?"

Dru was silent a moment, then laughed lightly. "Well, you have sorted me out, haven't you? If I speak, you'll be shocked at the shallowness of your sister's heart, I warn you!"

Dru leaned back and gazed at the ceiling, thinking.

"If I have been distant, it is only my jealousy at work again. Do you not know of what terrible emotions I am capable? Think of all these wedding preparations; not only you and Sebastian, but now Papa and Mrs. Tweetle. In two months I shall be the only one unmarried, and it is that which burdens me. Shall I become a decrepit spinster like Miss Lindstrom? What a frightening thought.

"And, I admit, the loss of yourself greatly weighs upon my mind. You've always been beside me, Rissa, and now you shall be gone. These are the petty troubles that plague me, and I'm sorry they have caused you concern."

None of which was a falsehood, thought Dru. Unless the omission of her greatest sorrow could be so counted. And that she was unwilling to share.

"You will never be like Miss Lindstrom!" Rissa said fiercely. "And you shall stay with Sebastian and me for as long as you like; all the time, if you so wish it. *I* should like it above all things, and I know he would as well. And he goes about in London society frequently; he has his house in town, and you must stay with us there and meet many eligible gentlemen. When we return from our wedding trip, won't you join us? Say you will!"

Dru had no desire to meet eligible gentlemen, but a plan was beginning to form in her mind, a plan borne of her own words.

"You go to Vienna in search of the followers of Mr. Mesmer, and such a search may take many months," Dru said. "I'm too impatient. I should like to be in London in time for the Little Season. I'm thinking of visiting Aunt Clara after the weddings. Papa will appreciate the time alone with Mrs. Tweetle, I should think."

Rissa exclaimed at the excellence of the plan and talked excitedly of new gowns, balls, and acquaintances which Dru must renew. It was some time before the younger lady could excuse herself to write the letter to Aunt Clara.

But it was not her aunt who received the first strokes of her pen that day. Bold though it might be, unladylike and forward as it was, Dru wrote her first missive to Duncan.

Earlier, she'd told Rissa the course of love never ran smoothly. She'd also reminded her to be true to her heart. How glibly the words had run off her tongue. But now they echoed through her own mind, haunting her with reproach. Could she overcome pride to heed their demands?

She could.

As the quill scratched across the paper, Dru saw Duncan's face before her. There was no need to recount his virtues; she knew them all. And he would expect the same strength of character in his wife. When she'd refused him because he was a footman, he perceived this as a flaw in her character.

The pen paused. *Does he expect perfection?* asked a small, angry voice. She tapped the feather against her upper lip thoughtfully. Duncan had forgiven her many things: she'd been rude to him; she'd accused him of kidnapping and stealing; had held him at gunpoint and wished him hung. Refusing his suit because he was a footman seemed minor in comparison.

But who knew the workings of the masculine mind! Mayhap she'd crossed a forbidden line. She seemed to recall her mother saying there were *some* things you never said to a gentlemen because he would be forever offended. Now she wished she'd paid more attention.

Whatever the reason, Dru was unwilling to let him fade away because of a misunderstanding. Pride could begone. She began to write again, telling him of her feelings and how they had undergone a change *before* she'd known he was a lord. How sad it had been, she wrote, that they'd not had the opportunity to discuss it before he left.

It was as far as she was willing to go, and a more brazen letter than she'd ever thought to send in her life. But it was all she knew to do; the result was in his hands. If he was shocked at her forwardness, if he didn't believe her, if he couldn't forgive—these would crush her, but at least the death of a promising love would not be her fault.

Trembling, feeling dreadfully vulnerable, she sealed the letter and began writing to Aunt Clara.

Less than an hour later Dru entered the hall. Rissa and Sebastian had gone for a drive, and only Jim Jacobs stood beside the library door. She hesitated a moment when seeing Jacobs; the poor man had experienced difficulties of late, but she must not display a lack of confidence in him. Besides, even he should be able to post a letter without mishap.

"Jacobs, take these letters into the village, please. I'd like them to go out on today's mail coach."

He bowed and put the letters in his pocket. "Yes, my lady," he said, barely disguising the bitterness he felt. Why were they always asking him to work when it was time for his kitchen break?

Deciding he deserved at least a slice of bread before leaving, Jacobs entered the kitchen. Several servants sat at table, and others stood talking in small groups while sipping coffee and devouring slabs of ham on bread that dripped with butter.

It was not fair.

Rebelliously, he filled his cup and made a sandwich. He sauntered toward the fire, where no one stood at present since Andre kept bobbing back and forth to stir the soup. Jacobs preferred to be alone of late, hoping to avoid company until his most recent error had died away in memory. Sighing contentedly, he took a large bite, a bite that soon tasted of ashes, for approaching him was one of the ones he wished to avoid.

"How goes it, Jim!" said Billy Ray, one of the larger groomsmen, and pounded him bruisingly on the back. "Tied up any lords lately?" Billy began to laugh unrestrainedly, a laugh which spread to others in the kitchen.

"Aw, leave 'im alone, Billy!" Jessup called from the table.

The groomsman patted Jacobs's back once more and walked away, still laughing. But the footman didn't care. His eyes were watching the fire in horror, for lying within it were Lady Dru's letters.

They must have fallen from his pocket when Billy knocked him on the back. So it wasn't his fault, but there was no doubting who'd get the blame for it. One of them was almost totally burned, the flames eating through the address even as he watched. The other was only singed at the corner.

He looked quickly behind him. No one appeared to be watching. Jacobs sank to his knees, laying his sandwich and cup on the floor. With careful fingers he plucked the letter from the fire and blew out the embers.

"Hey! What are you doing, you eediot?" Andre shouted, running toward him. "You don' feedle with my soup! No one touches Andre's creeashones!"

"Garn," Jacobs whispered, and slid the envelope up his sleeve without turning. When the heated paper came in contact with his skin, he rapidly stood to his feet. Beads of sweat moistened his forehead. "I-I'm not touching anything." He edged toward the servant's stair.

"You come back here, Jeem Jacobs, and clean theese mess you left," Andre demanded.

Jacobs shook his head. "Can't. Sick." And he fled up the stairs.

As soon as he was out of sight he removed the letter and fanned his sleeve. What could he do now? If he told Lady Dru he'd burned her letter, surely they would dismiss him. No one would understand his presence near a fire.

Could he simply not tell? Just mail the one letter and have done with it?

That would never work. With his luck, her correspondent would write and ask why she'd not written. He'd be found out, that was certain.

He closed his eyes and pictured the letter in the flames. It had been addressed to The Right Honourable Lord Kyle Duncan, a name that still gave him shivers when he recalled the man's anger as he bound him. What had the direction been? Number 12 Edward Street.

Now why had Lady Dru been writing *him?* It could only be to thank him for saving her sister's life. Such a letter was not beyond his abilities. He nodded his head in relief and hurried to his room.

His own stationery was not as fine as the lady's, but it would do. And he was capable of a fair imitation of her rounded, flowing handwriting; he'd seen it often enough on her letters.

"Dear Lord Duncan," the new letter began, "Thank you for saving Lady Clarissa's life. If my riting looks funny, it is because I have twisted my wrist."

Now, how would a lady twist her wrist? Jacobs wondered. If he didn't say, the lord might become suspicious. "I have twisted my wrist," the letter continued, "when embrodering." And thinking how ladies always gave great descriptions of clothing and material and such, he went on, "The cloth I am embrodering is very long. It is to cover a long piece of furniture. Maybe a church rail. It starts with leaves in each corner. Green, purple, red, and grey leaves ..."

* * *

A few days later, Lord Duncan stood in the hallway of his residence in London, leafing through the correspondence awaiting him. When he saw the return address upon one of the letters, his temples began to pound. Carelessly he threw the other missives back onto the salver and hurried toward his office, a room that had formerly served as a study before he'd converted the first floor to his investigative business.

"Carlisle!" he shouted.

"My lord?" the clerk inquired, running from his desk in the front room.

"Do not let anyone disturb me for awhile," Duncan said, and closed the door in his face.

"No, my lord," the plain, little man said earnestly to the wood.

Duncan opened the door. "And what's this 'my lord' business? Haven't I told you . . ."

Carlisle grinned. "Yes, sir. You have."

"All right then." Duncan closed the door again and sat at his desk. He held the letter tenderly within his hands, prolonging the moment of anticipation.

The past ten days had not been easy for Duncan. He'd been able to leave Druscilla with only the hardest firming of his heart. How the last sight of her bereft little face had haunted him! But he was a man of principle, or so he told himself. Lately, he'd had to remind himself of his principles on an hourly basis, so great was his desire to return to Brownworth-Selby Hall.

But how could he become shackled to a young lady who cared only for superficialities? Sure and she'd looked at him lovingly—when his true identity was discovered. There were many such young ladies available in parlours all over London.

But he'd hoped Druscilla was different. The love and

sacrifice she gave her sister hinted of an unbounded, loving nature. She was adventurous, fearless, and possessed just enough bite to her personality to save her from the insipidity so many maidens displayed.

But her refusal to marry him based upon his supposed low social rank had cut him to the core. How could he trust the depth of her love if it depended upon society's approval?

He stared at the letter in his hands and opened it slowly. Would it contain a message that could rekindle their courtship? Feeling the way he now did, it wouldn't require much.

Taking a deep breath, he began to read. And as he read, his eyebrows grew closer together in a terrible frown. When he had finished reading, he refolded the letter carefully and placed it within his breast pocket. Then, before the anger could fade, he took pen and paper and began to write.

Dru was at breakfast when Hayes entered with the morning mail. Lord Cathburn separated the missives. Dru accepted her letters, telling herself firmly not to hope; it was too soon to have a reply. But there, written in precise and elegant script, was Duncan's letter! Her heart raced. Surely such a timely answer showed the extremity of his emotion.

But she couldn't open it here, not with Rissa and Papa present. She excused herself and raced to the morning parlour. Sitting in her favourite armchair, she told herself to calm down. Then, with an admirable display of control, she opened the letter.

A few moments later, she re-entered the dining room. "I have received a message from Lord Duncan," she said brightly, her fists clenched within the folds of her dress.

A great plop of eggs landed on the tablecloth beside Lord Cathburn's plate, and he frowned up at the offending footman, who nervously scooped it away.

"Do be careful, Jacobs!" he scolded, then looked at his daughter. "What says Duncan?"

"Oh, not a great deal," she said airily. "Actually, it was a rather confusing letter." She forced a small laugh. "Something about hoping my embroidery was coming along well. And that he will be unable to attend the weddings, for he plans to visit Scotland straightaway."

The earl and Rissa expressed their disappointment in this, while Dru blinked rapidly and felt sick. But she was more determined than ever to tell *no one* of her hurt. The utter coldness of his letter had shocked her. How could he be so cruel? Even if he'd never cared for her, surely he could have shown some gentlemanly regard. Instead, he'd ignored her overtures entirely and had not bothered to hide his anger; indeed, every line shouted with cynicism.

Such a person was not worthy of her tender feelings. If he could not control his temper now, what would he be like in marriage? She should be grateful events had resolved in this fashion. But within moments the strain of feigning indifference took its toll and she excused herself once more.

The next weeks passed in a blur of activity. Trousseaus were made for Rissa and Dorothy, as Mrs. Tweetle had come to be called in their household; bridal gowns were commissioned; refreshments, music, flowers, invitations, decorations—all the details of weddings had to be selected and carried out.

Dru had no time to indulge her sorrow, though sadness numbed the joy she should be feeling. Yet it was impossible not to rejoice in Rissa and Sebastian's happiness, and to view her father and Dorothy's solicitous treatment of one another without pleasure.

It was impossible not to wish these things for herself.

But she carried on. She even came to appreciate Dorothy Tweetle, for that lady cared deeply for her father, and nothing could recommend her better to his daughter's favour. Dru had never seen him more contented.

The couples had decided upon a double ceremony, setting the date for the final week in September. Dru was to serve as their only attendant. The days and weeks stumbled by. Dru alternately wished for the weddings to be over and dreaded their arrival. But despite her wishes, or perhaps because of them, the week arrived at last.

Sebastian's mother came from London, and Rissa was pleased to find they got on well together. Dru found her somewhat stiff in manner and too formal for her taste, but Rissa could adjust to anyone.

Other friends and relatives arrived to fill the long-empty bedrooms of their house and those of the Winters's as well. Lord Mason and Lady Charity were among them.

The afternoon of the wedding was as fair as anyone could wish. Gentle breezes had swept the clouds from the sky and gave a poignant nip to the air. Perhaps it was this hint of fall which caused Dru's eyes to fill as she waited in the narthex of the church. Or it may only have been the mixed feelings she endured upon seeing her sister.

Rissa wore the tiara; Dorothy had decreed the honour should be hers since this was a second wedding for both the earl and herself. Rissa's gown was of ivory satin with an overlay of finely worked lace; tiny satin blossoms dotted the lace and the veil which flowed beneath the tiara. She was like a dream, and Sebastian a dream awaiting her in his formal black attire.

Before Dru walked down the aisle, she embraced **Rissa** lightly, careful of crushing their wedding finery and flowers.

"No one deserves happiness more," she whispered in Rissa's ear. "You are the dearest sister anyone has ever had. I love you!"

Rissa beamed, but Dru knew she had already left her. Her heart belonged at the other end of the aisle, where Sebastian gloatingly waited. Nevertheless, Rissa whispered back, "No, Dru, *you* are the dearest sister. And I love you as well. I pray you will soon know this happiness."

The earl pulled Rissa back into position. Dorothy, who held his other arm, watched them fondly. "You must go, Dru," he warned. "Sebastian looks to be in a notion to come back here and grab Rissa do you not hurry."

Dru smiled at him through a layer of tears. She looked at the three of them a final time and thought: *I must remember them as they are now. In later years, I must recall not my pain, but their joy.*

Dru and Aunt Clara remained at the Hall after the merry couples departed. Rissa and Sebastian traveled to Vienna, while Lord Cathburn and Dorothy crossed the channel to visit Paris. Dru wished to delay her own journey to London for several days to ensure that all returned to normal following the uproar of the past two months. There were a few lingering guests to accommodate beside.

When the last of the wedding visitors left, Dru still felt reluctant to depart. Aunt Clara, a little round mouse of a woman, was willing to remain as long as she wished. Everything was "pretty, so countrified and pretty," that she bustled outside for five-minute walks several times every day. Each outside venture kept her maid busy, for she would not leave without swathing her head in a large bonnet, pulling elbow-length gloves over her long-sleeved dress, calling for Hayes to assist her in putting on enormous, sturdy boots, and searching for her mischievous parasol.

She had not been so happy, she assured Dru, since she and Edmond and William had run about the grounds as children.

Dru would have been hard put to explain her reluctance to leave. The Hall was dreadfully lonely without Papa and Rissa. But somehow it suited her. It was a fitting accompaniment to her low spirits.

And here at the Hall, it was easier to indulge in her still-frequent bouts of weeping. Aunt Clara's house in Town was fashionable but small; her blue fits would be harder to hide there.

After accidentally observing several of her crying spells and being rebuffed when she offered her sympathy, Pizzy approached Jessup one evening after supper. She pulled him to one side of the kitchen where they could talk with some modicum of privacy.

"I'm worried about Lady Dru," she said. "Thought you might know what to do with the dear child, since you've got so many ladies about you."

"Aye, and I'll thank you for remindin' me," he sighed. "Though that lad Bradley has evened things a might, since he came to live with us. He's the match of four women, I can tell you that. What a jackanapes he is! But a real help with my squawlin' infants." He drank deeply of his ale. "So wot's this 'bout Lady Dru?"

"She cries and cries, like her heart's abursting."

"Well," he said consideringly, "she's probably missin' her kin."

"No, I think it's more than that. Tonight I opened the door real softly, and listened awhile." Seeing Jessup's expression, she blushed. "I wasn't being nosy, Karl! I thought I might learn something to help her. And," she glanced past Jessup's shoulder and lowered her voice, "I did hear her say Duncan's name. Do you think—is it possible—she could have liked him a little?"

Jessup shook his head. "Aw, Pizzy, I wisht you wouldn't ask me this kind of stuff. This is women's talk."

"Well, I'd have asked Martha if she weren't over the ocean right now," she said reasonably. "You know Lady Dru as well as anybody, Karl! What do you think?"

"Awright, awright," he said gruffly. "I reckon as it's possible, since they was together more than they should be. But if he's broke her heart, ain't much you nor I can do 'bout it."

A short distance away, Jim Jacobs put his cup of tea on the counter and stared at nothing. He knew it would come to this. He'd always known.

Do something wrong, his father had often told him, *do something wrong, and it will find you out. You will never be free.*

The past two months had passed in an agony of waiting to be caught. At first he'd been relieved to see his letter-writing had resulted in such a small ripple. Lady Dru had received a confused-sounding reply, that was all. He'd admonished himself for going overboard about the embroidery, but counted it a lucky idea anyway. He was still here, wasn't he?

But guilt had made him watch the young lady more closely than he'd ever done before. What if the letter she sent had *not* merely been a letter of thanks? And day by day, his fears seemed to be confirmed, for the young woman looked pale, wan, and spiritless. He could tell something was wrong.

And now, here was confirmation that something indeed *was* wrong. What if her letter had been a *love* letter? What if she'd answered a marriage proposal or something, and the baron thought she rejected him, writing on and on about embroidery?

What if she grew more and more sad until she died?

With his heart hammering in his ears, Jacobs marched up the stairs.

A few moments later, the entire kitchenful of servants ran upstairs, drawn by the sound of Lady Dru's screams.

12

Duncan looked at the enormous stack of mail on the hall table and sighed. Ten weeks was a long time to be gone, and almost he regretted ordering Carlisle not to send on his correspondence. But before going to his mother and Shanaleigh in Cromarty, he'd visited friends in Perth and Aberdeen and had fished in every river along the way, and his mail would have had a devil of a time finding him.

He picked up the first few messages, then threw them back on the pile. They could all be dealt with later. Just now he was tired from his journey and needed to rest. Shanaleigh, bless her, was eager for London entertainment, and expected him to escort her to the Lyceum this evening.

Not for the first time, he wondered at himself for bringing his high-spirited sister to England. He was a working man, after all, and had not the time to squire her about Town as she would want. He'd already been derelict in his duty as it was, running off because he did not wish to think about—but he still did not wish to think about *her*. Fortunately, he'd been between cases at the time, but who knew how many interesting puzzles he'd missed while he was gone?

Still, Shanaleigh would bring sparkle and life to his

house, which for some reason seemed more empty and dull than it ever had. He regretted his mother's not coming, for she could have entertained her during his absences. But knowing his sister, she would not be lonely for long.

He gave the stack of mail a final glance and turned away.

"You are so very, very pretty, Druscilla," Aunt Clara squeaked over the noise of other theatre-goers. "I'm glad you are not a big, tall thing like the young ladies try to be these days. There is no accounting for popular taste. My dear husband used to say a lady is known by her delicacy. Did you know they bind the feet of highborn ladies in China? Why should not considerate parents tie a weight uponst their daughter's heads to prevent unseemly height? Do you not think it a good idea, Druscilla?"

"What?" Dru removed her gaze from the milling crowd to focus upon her relative. "I'm sorry, what did you say?"

"Oh, nothing," the aunt replied, her lower lip protruding in a little pout. Her good spirits were becoming increasingly miffed by her niece's lack of attention toward herself. Clara had envisioned the two of them spending long, cozy afternoons and evenings at her house on Campden Hill. Instead, the child insisted they respond to every invitation, and if they had a rare night when no invitations were issued, they must go to Covent Garden or Drury Lane or, like tonight, the Lyceum. It gave her a fit of the shudders, it truly did, for these places were always burning down, everyone knew that.

And the entertainments! Faugh! She could do better herself. This evening, for example: Charles Matthews and his "Monodrama," or whatever he called it. Sitting at a table and pretending to be all the characters. What kind of nonsense was that? She knew she should imagine him as each new person, but all she could see was a grown man shouting and ranting and carrying on like a madman. She was glad it was over. If only their carriage would come! If only Druscilla would stop looking about like a loose woman!

Dru stopped looking. Finally, after weeks of hoping, she had found him. She knew Duncan would come back from Scotland sometime and that their paths would eventually cross. It was important to *see* him, in case he threw away her letters unopened. She would not blame him if he did such a thing. It's what *she* would have done, if Jim Jacobs had written to *her*.

And there he was at last, standing in front of the theatre, his strong features easily visible above the crowd. He was dressed in black evening clothes, a white silk shirt and cravat, and a black round hat. How urbane and handsome he looked.

And how lovely the lady on his arm.

Dru had never been fond of red hair, but she had to admit the colour seemed right for this female. It was a dark shade, having elements of brown mixed in, and did not subtract colour from her skin as brighter hues of red so often did. The young lady's hair was thick and curly and piled high atop her head. She wore a simple white satin gown and black spencer; her figure was tall and willowy and elegant, and she looked around her with bright, intelligent eyes.

Dru hated her at sight.

It certainly had not taken Duncan long to recover, Dru reflected, her brows lowering. Evidently *he'd* spent no time sobbing and sorrowing in his bedchamber mourning the loss of herself. He'd simply replaced her in the nonchalant way men seemed to do those things.

Well, she could have done the same. Gentlemen

seemed to notice her more this year, though whether it was the absence of Rissa or the interest the kidnapping story had aroused, she couldn't say. Yet she had been unable to generate any thought for other gentlemen.

But Duncan had no more allegiance than a cat. How he appeared to be enjoying himself! The look he gave the female was of tender amusement.

A sudden, horrible thought struck Dru. What if the woman was his *bride?* Mayhap he'd gone to Scotland to marry an old sweetheart!

Well, she was not one to stand about wondering. If she did not find out, she would spend hours and days in torture. Grabbing Aunt Clara's hand, she dragged her through the crowd.

Clara flapped her fan and reticule in confusion. "Druscilla!" she pleaded, "What—where—"

"I have seen an old friend you must meet!" Dru explained.

"But our carriage was next in line," moaned her aunt.

Duncan looked up from his sister's face, his vision drawn by a purposeful movement coming toward him. When he saw Dru, he felt the blood rush to his cheeks. His first inclination was to run, and he reached for Shanaleigh's arm and pulled; but there was nowhere to go without a conveyance, so he dropped his hand. Shanaleigh looked at her brother curiously, saw the direction of his gaze and its object, and became very interested.

Before Dru could open her mouth, Shanaleigh curtseyed and said, "You must be Lady Druscilla. I've heard so much about you."

"You—you have?" Dru asked in amazement, and remembered to curtsey back. She looked at Duncan, then rapidly away. Now that she stood before him, she wished she hadn't come.

He greeted her with stiff courtesy, then introduced his sister.

"Your sister?" Dru said gladly, then laughed. She acquainted them with her aunt. After the niceties were made, they stood in awkward silence, the crowd jostling around them carelessly.

Clara was near tears. Druscilla had jerked her all the way over here and away from her carriage just to stand like wooden poles beside these attractive young people. She wanted to be home, and she wanted to go to bed.

"I do so hate the theatre!" Clara wailed suddenly. "Don't you?"

Dru came to herself in a rush of shame. "Oh, Aunt Clara, I'm sorry!" She gave Duncan an apologetic look. "We must go."

And she hurried off, her arm circled protectively about her aunt's shoulders. As they entered the carriage, she could not resist a final glance at Duncan; she was both pleased and embarrassed to see he and his sister watched her with solemn attention. Dru gave them a nervous smile and disappeared into the coach.

For the rest of the evening she berated herself for not talking with Duncan about the letter. But what opportunity had there been? She didn't want to seem abrupt. Yet if she did not do something soon, the next lady on his arm might not be his sister.

Sitting in his office several days later, Duncan cursed himself for a fool. Ten weeks away from England. Ten weeks in which to form new memories and purge his mind of a certain beguiling young woman. And after less then ten minutes in her presence, his thoughts were once again in her bondage.

He stared at the letters on his desk. Two more letters

she'd written him since the one that had caused such pain. Two more chances to tease and stab his heart. He couldn't bear to open them.

What was she about that evening, coming to him like that? Looking so appealing and innocent; what a facade! He'd heard of such women; women who delighted in torturing a man's feelings. First they care, then they don't, then they do.

It was not a game he cared to play. Smoothing the letters carefully, he put them in his pocket and prepared to work.

Clara's eyes glazed as she watched the whirling dancers waltz past. It was the Wednesday evening ball at Almack's, and she had never been so bored in her life. Almack's was grossly overrated, she thought, though it would never do to admit it, since vouchers were so hard to obtain.

Here she sat in a big barren room with its wretched dance floor. Off to the side were smaller barren rooms with tasteless refreshments. They had nothing that she wanted to eat, anyway. And there were no flowers! Oh, why could there not be pretty flowers, to soften the eye?

Beside her sat no one interesting to talk with; only these gossiping, wrinkled old dowagers. Dru came over between almost every dance, but only for a twinkling, then off she'd go with another gentleman. Well, she'd been young once, too, but hopefully with more consideration to her elders. It was a long time ago, though, and maybe she hadn't been.

The waltz was ending and Dru looked at her now from the dance floor. Clara thought it wouldn't do for her to see how unhappy she was, so she gave a small, tight, *brave* smile, permitting her lips to tremble only the slightest amount. That should bring her.

But no, it wouldn't, for entering the room was that brother and sister they'd met at the Lyceum last week. And Dru approached them now, leaving her dance partner as though he didn't exist.

The child had the manners of a squirrel!

"I hope you're enjoying London," Dru was saying to Shanaleigh, and wishing she could think of something more original. If only she could speak with Duncan privately! His sister's lively eyes discomfited her. How much had Duncan told her?

"I'm liking London very much, thank you! Kyle is an excellent guide when he has time. We've seen the Tower and Hyde Park, and I hope to visit the Royal Circus next week."

The strains of the next dance began. "Well, come along, Shanaleigh, you have promised the first dance to me," Duncan said, and with a little bow to Dru, swept his sister away.

Dru's eyes narrowed contentiously. He was not making it easy. She watched him throughout the five figures of the quadrille, but not once did he look in her direction. When he rushed off with Shanaleigh afterward, she was not surprised at all.

Michael Warren, her partner for the next set, saw her observing their departure. "Isn't that Lord Duncan? The one who saved your sister?"

Dru, her eyes still on the door, admitted it was he.

"I don't care much for the Scots in general, but he's an exception, I suppose. O'course, he's half English, and that helps. His gorgeous creature of a sister don't hurt, either!"

Misinterpreting the look on her face he added gallantly, "Though she's no finer looking than you, Lady Druscilla! I'm sure my sister-in-law has invited them both to her ball next week. Do you join us?"

"Why yes," Dru decided, a gleam in her eye. "I do."

* * *

On Thursday evening of the following week, Duncan looked curiously at the footmen lining the hall of Dunstable Warren's town house. Each one held a long-stemmed rose. He could not help asking his host about it.

"Oh, the roses?" Mr. Warren laughed huskily. "Yon young lady is responsible. Cathburn's daughter. See her over there by the fireplace, in the green?"

The baron lifted eyes of dread in her direction. She was looking at him, as he knew she would be, and her face wore a tentative smile. He pretended not to notice.

"What a sweet thing to do," Shanaleigh said. "Why did she do it?"

Warren shrugged his shoulders and spread out his fingers. "Said she liked footmen; that's all I know!"

Shanaleigh gave her brother a mischievous look. "Oh, did she now? I want to talk with her."

"Well, I need to speak with Mr. Warren," Duncan said firmly. "You'll have to go alone. Mr. Warren and I have many things to discuss."

She observed Mr. Warren's surprised look and wrinkled her nose. "Very well, brave brother! I go alone!" She threaded her way across the crowded room. Dru watched her approach with a mixture of dread and anticipation.

After greeting Dru, Shanaleigh said, "What a charming gesture, giving the footmen roses. May I ask what prompted you to think of it?"

Dru had hoped Duncan would ask the question. It should have served as a conversational opening, if things had gone correctly. Instead, he stood with his back turned toward her. So she told his sister dispiritedly, "I have a fondness for footmen."

"Is that true?" Shanaleigh asked earnestly. "Because I have heard differently."

"You have?"

"Yes. It's been said that you are not sensitive to their lot in life. Nor the plight of others in similar situations."

Dru's ears throbbed. "I think that's a misunderstanding. One which I hope to correct."

Shanaleigh nodded. "When I first set eyes upon you, I suspected as much. I think some people stiffen their hearts and minds too quickly. They might even be so proud they carry old, hurtful letters in their pockets just to remind them not to relax their guard."

She moved closer to Dru, and whispered conspiratorially, "Women know better. They find it easier to forgive, because they have the good sense to know that pride makes a poor companion."

While Dru looked at her with wide eyes, Shanaleigh added, "I speak not to be disloyal to my brother, but to seek his happiness, which he is too stubborn to pursue himself. But I beg you, if your feelings are not truly engaged, do not continue to bring yourself to his notice."

Dru was so surprised by her frankness that speech failed her for a moment. She was also surprised to feel a sudden liking for this young woman with her strong sense of familial loyalty.

Realizing she awaited her answer, Dru began, "My feelings for your brother are not frivolous. I—"

"Oh!" Clara moaned from a nearby sofa. "Oh, my heart! It is beating too hard! Oh!"

Several people sitting beside the elderly lady jumped to their feet, and Dru rushed to her side. "What's wrong, Aunt Clara?"

"It is my heart," she said faintly, leaning her head back on the sofa cushion and giving Dru a pathetic glance. "I have not wanted to say, but it has been pounding and pounding lately. But . . . but I don't wish to trouble you, dear." Her voice dwindled to a whisper.

"You . . . you just go on, and enjoy yourself. I shall be . . . all right . . ."

"Don't speak nonsense! Shall we move you upstairs and call the physician?"

"No!" Clara exclaimed, then added weakly, "No . . . if I could just lie down in my own bed, I believe I should be all right in awhile. . . ."

Dru gave her a skeptical look, but she went to order the carriage. As she did so, she noticed Shanaleigh had rejoined her brother and watched her in sympathy, while Duncan became the only person in the room who did not observe their ignominious exit.

The next afternoon, Carlisle knocked at the door of Duncan's office. A young lady had come to inquire about a pair of stolen earrings, he said, but she would not leave her name. Would he see her?

Duncan had supposedly spent the last two hours poring over the plans of a new building's security measures, but for the longest time he'd merely stared at the knotholes in his desk and imagined they were roses.

He told Carlisle he'd be glad of the interruption.

Duncan stood when the young lady entered, looked up, then sat down again.

"Lady Druscilla!" he said in dismay. He stood up once more. "I—I was just leaving. There is an emergency."

Dru glared at him, walked around the desk, and pushed her hand against his chest. "I have been trying to speak with you for three months," she said angrily. "I have written; I have worn my aunt into a nervous frenzy attending every function in Town in the hopes of seeing you; and I have discommoded twenty footmen who had better things to do with their hands than hold flowers;

all in futile attempts to speak with you. And now you dare to tell me you are leaving?"

Duncan sat down. His eyelid began to twitch. "I—I suppose I can spare a few moments."

Dru nodded once and returned to the other side of the desk. She sat in the client's chair and folded her arms.

"I did not write that note," she said.

Duncan tilted his head. "What note is that?"

"The one you carry within your pocket." When she saw his cheeks redden and his eyes flash, she nodded in satisfaction.

"Someone has been speaking out of turn," he said in a dangerous voice.

"Perhaps. But do not blame her. The point is, I did not write that note. Do you remember once saying those words to me?"

"I recall it, and how you did not believe me when I said them."

"But how wrong I was. Do you remember how quickly I did believe you, though? After you spoke with me?"

He paused and looked away. "I can't imagine that we have anything to speak about."

"That is because you are obstinate." When he frowned, she added quickly, "But I shan't let that stop me. Duncan, Jim Jacobs wrote the note you carry."

"Jim Jacobs!" he laughed. "Oh, Druscilla. If you are going to make excuses, you must do better than that!"

"Duncan," she said firmly, "you do recall how prone to error the man is. Remember how he hit you over the head with a chair and tied you up?"

Duncan's laughter began to fade. "Yes, I won't soon forget it."

"Well. Shortly after you left the Hall three months ago, *without explanation,* I might add, I wrote a letter to you and asked Jacobs to mail it in the village. Somehow, in the execution of this small duty, he accidentally burned the letter. Fearing he'd be dismissed, he elected not to tell me, but to write another in its place. It is that which you carry."

Duncan studied her face for a long moment, considering. It would be just like the footman to do such a foolish thing. Suddenly he felt a band loosen around his chest; a band he'd not known was there.

"Truly?" he asked.

"Truly."

Keeping his eyes riveted on hers, he said, "Jacobs waxed eloquent about hurt wrists and embroidered cloths in *his* letter. What did you write in *yours?*"

She dropped her eyes. "Oh . . . I wrote about how sad it was that you left before I could tell you something very important."

"And what was that?"

"How my feelings had changed," she said, her voice quivering. "At the Old Hall that day, before we arrived home, before I knew you were a lord, I suddenly realized that it didn't matter after all if you were a footman." She lifted her eyes. "Nothing was important . . . except loving you."

When the silence lengthened, she looked down at her hands. "Of course, you may not believe me."

Duncan felt the final bands breaking across his heart. "Druscilla Selby," he said, and rose to walk around the desk, "when have I ever not believed you?"

He pulled her to her feet.

Dru's heart beat so quickly she thought it might explode. After all her boldness, she was too shy to look at him. Duncan placed his fingers beneath her chin and turned her face upward, forcing her to meet his eyes. He looked at her with humour, warmth, and something more which caught the breath in her throat.

"Why didn't you tell me sooner?" he murmured, a twinkle in his eye. "We have lost all this time."

Before Dru could make an indignant response, his lips met hers in a kiss that lifted her off the floor and into his arms. Laughing, they spun about the room as he held her, until they became dizzy and collapsed upon the sofa. Unwilling to be separated from her for even a moment, he pulled her onto his lap.

"I'd forgotten what it is to have you in my arms," he said. "How I love you! I regret leaving so abruptly all those months ago. Though I must admit my misconceived disappointment in you was not the only reason I ran away; partly it was my sense of shame in nearly losing Clarissa."

"But it wasn't your fault, Duncan. How could you have prevented it, when you were caught beneath the wardrobe?"

"Had I been more alert in entering my room, that overwrought footman would not have knocked me over the head. Even worse, my men panicked and looked for me instead of watching Clarissa." He shook his head. "I thought they were better trained than that."

"Something much worse might have happened if James had abducted her another time."

"Mayhap. Still, if things had not gone so far, I'd not have the burning of that fine ship on my conscience. But we were outnumbered, and there appeared no way of avoiding it. At least there was no great loss of life, other than Burke."

Dru saw from his face that even that death had been too much. Softly she said, "You are a strong man, Duncan, but a gentle one. When we are wed—" Her face flushed crimson, and she stopped.

"Yes?" Duncan said, his eyes teasing. "What was that you said? Something about a wedding?"

She glared at him. "It has only just occurred to me

that you have not—that is . . . oh, bother it! Do you not mean to ask me, then? For if not, I've chosen the wrong seat in this room and will move immediately."

His arms grew heavy about her waist, and he hid his face in her hair. "And I thought you were just glad to see me."

"Kyle Duncan!"

Laughing gently, he turned her face to his. "Druscilla, my love," he said, his mouth achingly close to hers, "will you be my wife?"

Dru stared in fascination at the graceful curves of his lips. "Yes," she whispered. "I will."

After a long, pleasurable interval, Duncan demanded, "How long before your father returns from his wedding trip?"

"Within the month."

"It is too long. We must go to Scotland and be wed immediately."

"Oh no," Dru said. "I'm anxious too, dearest, but I want Rissa and Papa in attendance. I'd also like time to know your sister and meet your mother.

"Besides," she added, and moved her eyebrows expressively, "a Selby woman is not truly wed lest she wears the tiara."

Duncan groaned. "And thus we come to the real reason you wish to marry. To wear that cursed crown."

She giggled. "No, the true reason is to take you away from all this."

"Away?" He looked at the room curiously. "From all this?"

"Yes! Duncan, do you know that my wedding portion could be accounted a fortune? You shall not have to work! We can refurbish your estate, reinforce your castle walls, whatever you like!"

He shifted, moving her not off his lap, but slightly apart. "Have you learned nothing about me? Druscilla,

I do not *need* to work, even without your fortune. I'm not impoverished! But neither am I able to sit idle in the country. I do investigations because I enjoy it."

"But ... as I started to say earlier, you are a gentle person. You felt the death of James deeply, I know you did, even though he was a bad man. Surely this kind of work will lead you to similar situations—*dangerous* situations, where you must hurt someone, or—" her eyes widened, "or even worse, be injured yourself."

Pulling her close, he said, "It is the rare case which is dangerous. Much of what I do goes unnoticed. I search for motives, Druscilla, and it is most intriguing what one can learn of humanity. And sometimes, if one is fortunate, there is the satisfaction of preventing injustice."

"If your work is so free from danger, then," she said rebelliously, "you won't mind if I help you."

"Help me?"

"Yes, and do not look so amused. I like to investigate things, too, you know. Didn't I almost discover your identity?"

"You came to the conclusion I was a kidnapper, if I remember correctly."

"I shall be more careful in my conclusions next time."

Duncan looked at her warily.

Fortunately for him, Carlisle chose that moment to knock. Confident of his welcome, the clerk did not wait for his employer to reply before opening the door. When he saw the pair on the sofa, however, he immediately withdrew, his face white with shock.

"I wonder what he wanted," Dru said.

"He'll be resigning do I not explain things," Duncan chuckled. "By the way," he added, eager to deflect her mind from investigations, "whatever became of that footman? Did you send him packing?"

"Jacobs? No, I had not the heart. He always means well. But I made him promise that should he have any helpful ideas in the future, he must ask Hayes or my father first."

Duncan threw back his head and laughed. Kissing the tip of her nose, he said, "Forget about investigations, little one. You have a promising future in diplomacy!"

We shall see about that, Dru thought to herself, but she gave him a delicious smile and moved closer to his lips.

"Yes, my lord footman," she whispered.